Gennita Low

Summer Fire (Hot Spies 1 & 2)
Copyright © 2017 Gennita Low
Cover by HOTDAMNDesigns
ISBN-13: 978-0-9914742-1-9

PUBLISHER'S NOTE
This book is a work of fiction. Names, characters, places, and incidents either are the product of the author's imagination or are used fictitiously, and any resemblance to actual persons, living or dead, business establishments, events, or locales is entirely coincidental.

The publisher does not have any control over and does not assume any responsibility for author or third-party Web sites or their content.

Published by: GLow World

A GLOW WORLD PRODUCTION

SUMMER FIRE
Hot Spies 1 & 2

by

GENNITA LOW

Also by Gennita Low

~ ~ Children's books as "Gennita" ~ ~

A SQUIRREL CAME TO STAY

DANGEROUSLY HOT

(Hot Spies 1)

by

Gennita Low

To Father and Mother

Ranger Buddy, hot and sweaty

Stash, my hottie

Dedicated to all the warriors, those in the crossfire,
who bravely served or are serving.

Special thanks to Melinda Hutchenrider.

CHAPTER ONE

Outskirts of Tallinn, Estonia

The man was delicious to look at. What Americans would call "hot." Tall. Dark-haired and rakish-looking with that stubble. And, as always, that heated look in his jewel-green eyes gave her a sudden need for a long cool drink, preferably with vodka.

She was long past the point of wondering why he affected her this way. He just did. At each meeting, she anticipated his gaze, so direct, so damn intimate, and each time, she couldn't help herself. She winked at him. And then, depending on the situation, they would pick up or exchange items in the middle of the place or one of them would back away, following the unspoken protocol of a first-come-first-serve basis.

It was part of the game. She could play it a bit hotter but knew she couldn't afford it. It was just too bad they were on opposite sides because she had a feeling it'd be more than a bit hotter.

Scorching, more like.

Her superiors wouldn't approve any consorting without their say-so. After all, she was their fixer. She couldn't be seen being friendly with someone who could use it against her.

But damn, he was hot. She waited for him to step back, do his usual two finger salute to acknowledge that she'd arrived first this time, but instead, he started walking slowly toward her.

She frowned. This wasn't their pattern. Nowadays, their respective agencies had agreed to do things with the least casualties as possible. Yes, some treaties actually included secret clauses like "first-come-first-serve," "positional operative compromise" and "negotiable exchange."

So civilized.

She didn't back away as he approached. Curiosity stopped her. He had a hand in his jacket, probably a weapon. It occurred to her she might be a target but she didn't think so. If he'd wanted to kill her, he'd have done so already from five meters away. Or any number of times she'd bumped into him the last ten or so months.

They'd never spoken to each other directly. He'd never touched her. Their long looks at each other had been when there were no witnesses.

She watched, unable to move, as his hands came up and cupped her face. Tilted it up. His thumbs rubbed her cheeks. She didn't do a thing as his head swooped down and his lips caught hers. His tongue swept into her surprised mouth. Tangled. Tasted. Vodka and lime. Five seconds, tops.

He stepped back and gazed down at her, those eyes cool and unreadable. The corners of his lips lifted slightly, a smile of a man who had just discovered a secret.

"I've wanted to do that for a while now," he softly said, that husky American Southern twang sending a tingle down her spine.

That voice was distinct, instantly recognized in the European underground. The Cowboy had a reputation of getting things done his way. But she had a reputation too, a lethal one.

She continued watching him as he disappeared into the shadows. Five seconds could get a man killed. Five seconds could change one's life.

* * *

"So, did you make your move?"

Luke unzipped his leather jacket, shrugged out of it, and hung it on the hook by the entrance. His friend, Konstantin, continued regarding him from the small dining table as he walked to the fridge. Perusing his options, he closed it, and went for hard liquor instead. He went to sit across from his flat mate. He took a swig from the bottle.

Konstantin flapped the newspapers, folding it over, his dark eyes mocking him with a knowing gaze. "Was she that good? Or that bad?"

Ignoring Konstantin was pointless. He'd just continue riding him all night.

"Maybe I didn't see her," Luke said.

"And maybe cows don't fly. You have the lovesick look about you, buddy."

Luke grinned. Konstantin's trademark of over-the-top exaggeration was just what he needed to loosen the tension inside him. His frustration must really be showing. Konstantin had that "I got you pegged" look in his eyes. "Pigs. It should be 'and maybe pigs fly.' Cows already don't fly, Kostya."

"*Whatever.*" Konstantin copied the popular American slang term with bored perfection. He flicked his hand expressively. "You're changing the subject. You can't distract me from my quest."

His flat mate also loved online role-playing games. His current obsession was some medieval quest for magical weapons that pitted worldwide players against each other. Luke had watched him at his gaming sessions now and then, although it was beyond him why anyone, let alone someone who was in their business, would play a multi-level dungeon and dragons game for months on end without getting bored.

When asked, Konstantin had just shrugged and replied that it kept him on his toes, and besides, he met interesting people, from professors of medieval history to young men bored with their current factory jobs. Luke supposed those types were interesting to his friend only because they were ordinary people living safe, ordinary lives. He was so into it, he'd brought his current gaming character, Sir Constantinus, into his real-life dialogue, both amusing and somewhat disconcerting to some.

Luke took another swig and peered over the bottle. "And your quest is?"

"Come on, we all deal with information. Do you know how much I could get for proof that The Cowboy and *La Niña* are sitting on a branch?"

"In a tree," Luke corrected and frowned. "I should've known you'd try to sell information like that."

Konstantin snorted. "You don't care if I do or I don't. The ladies think The Cowboy is a handsome challenge anyway."

Luke hadn't chosen that nickname. They called him that because he was so obviously American, with his South Georgia drawl and his boots. It was a pretty useful one since it didn't sound particularly threatening and was easily identifiable. It didn't take too long for many in the underground network to get to know the name and it was the first one on their minds any time they needed something fixed that needed an American handler.

Exactly what he wanted. Information from the fringe. Non-network news.

As for *La Niña*, the woman given that handle of the cold front which swept through the oceans, was neither a child or frigid. In fact, she was all woman and smoldering hot.

"You know, your silence is louder than any rock concert." Konstantin reached for his own drink. He cocked an eyebrow before tipping his head back. "You didn't get any."

Luke laughed. He certainly wasn't going to divulge any more information than necessary. "You have it all figured out, Kostya."

"She's *La Niña*. She may have a positive effect on masculine parts but that icy attitude wilts everything. And," Konstantin added, "she beat you to the place first. Again. How many times this year already?"

"Not that many." Six to be exact. Out of the dozen or so times they'd gone after the same thing, they'd somehow arrived at almost the same time. She'd scowled the first couple of occasions when he'd beaten her by those crucial seconds, but the very first time she'd gotten the best of him, he'd been rewarded with a sexy smile and a kiss blown in his direction. It was the first smile he'd ever seen on her lips and it lit up her usually guarded eyes.

No, he was convinced that icy attitude about which everyone was so turned off was fake. He'd seen amusement in her eyes before and she'd given him enough saucy winks, betraying a hidden side of her.

Everything about her intrigued him. He had too much going on to make any move, but she often invaded his thoughts. Too much.

When they'd first met, he'd been amused by the icy wall of disdain the dark beauty had thrown up at him and everyone around. She'd looked as if she had better things to do with her time than mixing around with a bunch of politicians. He hadn't blamed her. It was a boring affair, with lots of standing around and hand clapping after long, pompous speeches.

It was only an hour or two later, when they'd "bumped" into each other while crawling in the ventilation system, that he'd realized she wasn't just arm candy for some wealthy contributor. They'd paused without any startled movements, as if it was quite normal to meet in cramped spaces in between building floors, and she'd cocked her head and studied him for a few seconds before whispering in accented English, "I'm going *that* way."

She'd pointed to a different direction from his. He'd nodded and replied, "Have fun," before moving on. Different agendas. He hadn't thought she would report him.

That was the night he'd asked Konstantin to get him a file on her. Since then, he and the delectable *Niina*, as everyone called her, had "bumped" into each other in Macedonia, France, Switzerland, even Morocco. It was always interesting how different she looked and acted each time, yet the look she always gave him had the same intriguing amusement. She'd also managed to not have any direct contact with him. Most fixers knew and contacted each other for favors and exchanges of information. From Konstantin's file, "*La Niña*" didn't do that much.

Until now, he hadn't really acted on his attraction. But it'd been a week of frustration. He'd thought he'd found the most promising lead and it had led to nowhere. His disappointment, after months of continual failure, was bitter medicine. Tonight he'd gone out to make some money to pay for the recent expenses and there she was, beating him to the job. So, at the spur of the moment, he'd decided he needed a consolation prize.

Luke frowned. With as much travel as he did, they shouldn't have met that often. Unless—Konstantin's exaggerated sigh interrupted his reverie.

"You should really ask more questions about her," his friend said, flapping his papers again.

Luke raised his eyebrows. "Are you offering it for free? That file you sold me cost a fortune."

"Hey, I need to pay bills too, you know. And the landlady raised the rent."

"I gave you extra rent money," Luke pointed out.

"Only for the time you're staying here. What about when I'm all alone to fend for myself?"

He laughed and took another drink. Konstantin made enough money but spent too much on high-tech games and gadgets.

"Tell you what," he said. "I'll cover next month's rent if, and only if, you have good information, something that tells me what her handlers are after. We've been around the same places too much lately. I can't see how my project ties in with her people's interests. Find me something that gives me a clue."

Konstantin smiled wickedly. "Done." He pulled a disk from between the pages of his newspaper. "Your wish is my command. Those who seek will find."

Luke scratched his stubble with the bottle's mouth. He should've known Konstantin had something up his sleeve. He reached for the disk.

His friend shook his head and laid a hand over it. "Uh-uh. First, we agree on the month's rent?"

"Only if the information is useful."

"You know, if you weren't a friend, I'd just take the disk back and let you find yourself another sifter. Most people just pay and take what is there."

"That's flea market information. You're a specialist."

"Why, thank you."

"Not that your sifting skills have helped me in *my* quest the last ten months," Luke said. Every piece of information Konstantin had provided had led to dead ends or more questions. It was time to push his friend a bit harder. "Maybe it's beyond your skill level?"

"Ouch. You wound me. And I suddenly feel insulted. You're lucky you have a bottle in front of you or I might not fight the urge to punch you."

Luke grinned back mockingly. "Now you're trying to distract me. I don't dispute your amazing ability to get news about lost objects, but maybe missing people isn't your forte."

Konstantin was a first-rate sifter and in spite of recent setbacks, Luke was confident he would eventually dig up a key piece of information that would help. But, he'd also kept the real reason why he'd kept on going from Konstantin, in spite of depleted funds and numerous dead ends. Ten months missing was a long time, but he refused to give up.

"Yet you're curious enough about *La Niña* you asked me to assemble a file for you. Technically, she isn't a missing object or person, so how do you know my info is correct?" Konstantin mocked back. He pushed the disk across the table. "Do you want this or not?"

"You're a pain in the ass when you're argumentative."

"And you're cute when you're mad. Now come on, let's do some good drinking. That woman's obviously gotten under your skin. Either you get laid or she's going to make you a bad-tempered poor man."

Luke agreed. He'd barely tasted her. He wanted to do more.

Later, after another hour of shared alcoholic small talk, he sat at his desk in his room. Konstantin had tried to play down the lack of new avenues, advising him something unexpected always appeared. Trying to avoid thinking about his disappointment and a certain hot kiss, he'd drunk quite a bit more than he'd wanted, until Konstantin had checked his watch and abruptly sent him to bed, joking that he should go dream about *La Niña*.

Oblivion would be welcome. Curiosity got the better of him, though. He inserted the disk into his laptop and started clicking on the objects in the open folder. A personal email. Familiar items they'd both gone after. One was an envelope she'd gotten hold of before him. Photos. Probably blackmail ones. Fixers generally were asked to retrieve those. He clicked on one of the thumbnails. The image made him sit up in his chair, the warmth from alcoholic consumption receding like a bucket of ice water.

"Damn you, Kostya," Luke muttered. His friend had played him well.

* * *

Tonight's job was relatively simple. Pick up an envelope at the old hotel's desk. Deliver it. No dressing up. No taking off to another country. Nothing strenuous, unlike the last assignment, that had included scaling a building in the dead of night. The meeting was going to take place at a much later hour, giving her time for a quick meal.

Looking out the bus window, Nina rubbed the back of her neck. Easy night but then, it wasn't over yet, and she was still tired. She needed some downtime soon. Traveling all over the place meant little time to adjust to different time zones. She'd been making do with naps but her energy wasn't at peak level. Not good. She needed to be on her toes at all times. She might be called *La Niña* after the wind, but currently, she felt neither quick nor powerful.

Tonight, she'd slipped, allowed her curiosity to get the better of her. *Cowboy.* That name whispered through her mind, fanning a memory like a warm summer breeze. She'd already let him get to her, and now she'd gone one step further. Why had he kissed her? That was the last thing she'd expected—him acting out her fantasy.

14

She must be tired. Or she would have given him a reason or two not to touch her again. She felt her lips involuntarily curve into a smile thinking about him. He did look good in that leather jacket, though. She'd wanted to put her hands inside it to find out whether he was as hot as he looked. Her smile turned into a grin which she hastily hid with a hand, pretending to suppress a yawn.

She stood up as the bus neared her destination. Good-looking or not, she couldn't afford any distractions right now, and especially with someone in this business. Things were murkier than ever and adding another emotional complication into her life would be exactly like the little missteps that led to a fatal one. Of course, her father was referring to chess pieces she lost to him one by one during their games, but she'd always known he was teaching her something else entirely.

A cold blast of air hit her as she exited. Exactly what she needed.

She walked briskly down the winding streets, the old crumbling cobblestones under her shoes sticky with wet dirt and trash from the day. There weren't too many people out at this hour but no one was ever alone in this part of town. The tourists had gone back to their hotels, warned by their guides to stay away at night; most of the locals avoided the area, knowing well it could erupt in sudden violence in the darkness of night; and the law, paid off, mostly looked away. The result was an area on the seedy side of the town that was mostly self-governed by crime groups.

Some, like her, had a pass to walk through without too much fear of being accosted by gangs. Nina kept one hand in her jacket, though. It didn't pay to be complacent.

In the daylight the old city had the charm of history mixed with modern high rises, but late at night, parts of it became gothic, shrouded with secrets. The underground world came alive. Cobbled alleys and ancient arches led to sweaty clubs playing techno music and forbidden back ways that opened to other forbidden dens of iniquity. This was where things got exchanged without being traced, where deals were made between parties preferring to stay anonymous, and where those playing international espionage games sometimes chose to meet. Tallinn was a city churning with foreigners and Nina knew she was thought of as just another person seeking her fortune between the borders of Russia and Finland, as so many had done throughout the centuries.

She rapped three times at the door of a massive structure that had been the house of a nobleman a century ago. Now it was run by people not quite as noble. Nina suppressed another smile. Something was wrong with her tonight. She couldn't seem to stop joking about every little thing.

A little hole slid open and a face peered out. "What's the problem?" he asked in Russian.

The code word was "found." "I found something you lost," Nina replied, "and would like to return it to the owner."

The slider shut and the door unlocked with a loud clack. She pushed it open with a foot. A big burly man sat at a high round table, playing solitaire, a gun by a stack of cards. He didn't look up.

"Left passage, second door. Don't go in anywhere else or you deal with the consequences."

Nina strode into the dingy foyer. She placed cash on the table, right beside the weapon.

"Relax, Mikhail," she drawled. "I've never caused any trouble here."

The burly man turned over a card. "Keep it that way. I like you, *La Niña*, but there've been reports you used your weapon in the market place. I don't want any attention drawn here."

Nina shrugged. "The market place is different. Everyone's trigger happy and thinks with his dick." Her persona, *La Niña*, was a cold and unapproachable character and she played that part well. Fuck with *La Niña* and she used her weapon. It was a good way to keep the hooligans at bay. She looked in the direction of the left passage. "Is the owner here or do I wait?"

"Not here yet." Mikhail finally looked up. His eyes, mismatched in size, made him sinister- and dangerous-looking even without the gun. "I wouldn't dawdle with this one. Whatever you're up to, finish with him quickly."

"Didn't think you cared," she murmured. Behind those doors were clandestine meetings going on. The man sitting there didn't look it, but he had good information.

Mikhail picked up her cash and pocketed it. His gaze met hers, dark and emotionless. "Nah," he said. He pointed a beefy finger to his bald head. "Just wanted you to think about who you're dealing with. Money is everything but some money takes everything."

Nina held his gaze for a moment. Warning?

"That's a roundabout way of saying money isn't everything," she retorted lightly. "I absolutely agree. I'll talk to you later."

She went to the designated room, a simple small 5x5 place with a table, chairs and a jug of water. It was actually one of the more "luxurious" rooms in the building. She'd been inside a couple that were cubby holes, not unlike confessional booths in churches, except those using them were probably planning to commit more sins rather than to repent.

She picked the chair facing the door. Five minutes passed. Usually, they were on time or her handler would call her on her cell. Ten minutes. Her rule book said, if there were no communication, an item not picked up went back to the open market at her discretion. Patting her jacket, she thought of the large envelope hidden inside. She didn't know what was in it and should first call to ascertain everything was in order. Missed meetings were not a usual thing. She stood up.

Nina nodded at Mikhail, giving him a shrug as information. He checked the monitor on the wall, pulled a lever and the heavy wooden door unlocked. Outside, she zipped her jacket up again as she slipped into the semi-darkness.

Across the street, a group of youths were dancing as their thug friends jeered on. Down the road, she could see prostitutes sitting on their stools under some brightly lit corridors. Parked cars. No one hurrying toward the building. She cast a furtive glance to her right. She took a side alley. Down another. She finally turned around.

"You're a lousy tail," she remarked conversationally. "I usually shoot first when I'm tired. You'd better come out, Cowboy."

He emerged from behind, much closer than he should be.

His voice floated toward her, dark with promise. "I'm much better on top."

CHAPTER TWO

Luke had caught the car keys Konstantin had thrown in his direction as he'd hurried out of the flat. He'd ignored the grin of triumph thrown at him. There hadn't been time to stop to cuss his friend out for the deliberate delay. As it was, Konstantin had timed the whole incident, cutting it very close. Barring any accident, he might miss her—damn it, Kostya, this wasn't an online game. Luke was very aware that he'd just shown his hand on how important the information was by practically running off without a word.

Never mind that he'd arrived with just enough time to wait for *La Niña* to conduct her business. He'd drunk enough to know he was acting more on emotion than reason. There hadn't been much time to plan and here she was, strutting about in the back alleys of Tallinn like she owned the place.

A woman of experience would know she was being followed. He didn't bother being too covert. She had something he wanted.

"Twice in one night, Cowboy?" The mockery in her voice was obvious.

He didn't want to flirt. He had questions that needed immediate answers. But the vodka had relaxed his mood, addled his usual caution. Right now, he felt more himself than he'd been for months.

"Or more," he said, "if needed."

Her laughter echoed softly in the darkened alley. "Tempting. But the night's almost gone. Why are you here, tailing me?"

He suddenly realized she was speaking with an American accent. He shouldn't be surprised. He'd heard her with different ones—thick French, slurred Russian, broken English. The woman had a gift with languages, which pretty much covered most of the citizens in this part of the world.

"I've business that can't wait."

"You knew where to find me. I'm curious. How?"

"Lady, this is our job, remember? Besides, maybe I have business inside the same place."

She approached. In this darkness, with that bottle of vodka swirling in his brain, his other senses seemed to have taken over. Her every movement stroked him like soft velvet. He needed to implement a plan quickly or he was going to lose it.

"Our business seems to be crossing paths a lot," she murmured. "Ever since that night in Nice, in fact."

He took a step closer. Another, and he would have her against the wall. He breathed in, instinctively seeking her scent. She always smelled good to him, a subtle combination that reminded him of home.

"Exactly," he said. "I think it's time we get further acquainted."

Again, she laughed, sending a delicious shiver down his back. He was feeling amazingly reckless.

"Cowboy—"

Hell. Caution be damn. "Luke," he interrupted. "Let's start with calling me Luke. I'd like to call you...Naya."

Her sharply drawn breath gave him that one moment of advantage. Although not at 100 percent, he'd anticipated her attack. He dodged the fist. She grabbed his jacket and pulled. Turning, he sidestepped the knee to the groin. The jab to the back of his thigh brought his focus back.

Finesse was fine. But brute strength was far superior. His years in the rodeo circuit had been useful in this business in unexpected ways.

Twist. A snap of her arm—he was careful not to break it—and he had her front against the stone wall. She wasn't giving up easily, though, moving her leg between his to try to break his hold.

He pressed harder, burying his face against her ear. Her scent invaded and he breathed in deeply. "Tell me, what perfume is that?"

That unexpected question stopped her struggling. Her pause gave him the extra second to secure her even more tightly under him. He wrapped his legs around hers, gripping her with his thighs like he would a bucking steer. Her ass felt good where it was.

She sniffed. "You're drunk!"

"A bit. See, I'm no danger to you. Just wanted to get better acquainted. Want to answer a few questions?"

"Go to hell."

Somehow he knew she wouldn't be that cooperative. Her ass wiggled, rubbing in a way that just wasn't conducive to calm questioning. He had things he needed to ask and all he could think of was turning her around and tasting those fine lips again.

"This isn't quite the venue I had in mind, though," he said.

Some things he could do blindfolded. Like securing a trapped calf. He reached for his back pocket. Timing was everything. He made quick work of making her his prisoner. Her strangled sound of outrage was choked off by a gag. Her hands reached up to undo it and he cuffed her easily. When she swung around, he squatted, jerking the chain on the cuff to unbalance her. She toppled over his waiting shoulder and he secured her ankles with ties. Not bad. Almost like old times.

"Sorry about this, but I can't have you screaming murder while I take you back to my car." He put her back on her feet and reached inside his jacket. He had a hood in one of the pockets. He slid it over her head, with the eyeholes on the wrong side so she couldn't see. "Can't have you recognized either."

Luke swung her over his shoulder again and strode out of the alley. At this hour, walking in public with an abducted female would hardly lift an eyebrow.

"Don't wiggle like that, sweetheart. I don't want to spank you."

He had a pretty good idea the names she was calling him behind the gag. He was drunk and reckless and he didn't care. He laid one hand on her cute ass and gave it a warning squeeze. She froze.

* * *

Nina was too angry to be afraid. The hood disoriented her. She couldn't tell which direction they were heading. No one stopped them—why would they? At this hour, crimes are committed all the time.

Questions raced through her mind. How did he know her name? What did he want? They'd bumped into each other enough times that she'd let down her guard. Was that his plan?

It didn't matter. He knew her name. How much did he know about her?

The hand lightly gripping her ass was distracting too. It felt hot there. Spank her. She was going to—no, she'd to control her temper and think clearly.

A fixer like him delivered or exchanged things—was she part of a deal? The sound of a car door being opened brought her attention back to her problem at hand. When he shifted his hold on her to get her inside the car, she lifted her tied legs and kicked blindly in his direction, hoping to make contact. Damn. He moved pretty fast for a drunk.

"Really don't want to stuff you in the trunk—I mean, boot—so don't tempt me."

There was a short pause, then she felt her legs being hoisted up, higher than seat level. Something pulled them to one side and wound around her calves several times, locking them to the seat. A familiar click. Just like that, he had her strapped down by a seat belt. She tugged fiercely but it was impossible to move without being able to see.

"Just be patient," he told her, tugging the belt here and there. She had never felt so helpless. "There, all snug and comfy. You'll be out of this soon."

Soon? *Soon?*

He sounded so damn soothing she wanted to throttle him. After she'd tied him up first and...and...*think, Naya, think*. This was no joking matter. What was he up to? She tamped down the little niggle of fear starting to grow. No, none of that. She would get out of this jam somehow and get back to finishing what she'd started. He was drunk but very strong. Drunk meant she could get to him in other ways, though. Could she seduce him, maybe?

The car started moving. He began whistling softly, clearly enjoying himself. Nina gritted her teeth. Strike seduction. Instead, she thought of ways to kill him as he drove.

* * *

Luke glanced over at his prisoner, now sitting quietly, all secured by the safety belt and his cuffs. He didn't think she'd fallen asleep. His plan, hastily formulated, was effective in the sense that he didn't have to ask around for her and getting her handler's attention. He could have done that, but he might decide to play the usual cloak and dagger games and he'd lost his patience. Time was running out.

Konstantin's latest information appeared like a lifeboat to someone stranded at sea. All these months and nothing. She—he glanced at her again—was probably his last chance to find out what happened to Drei. The date on the disk made her probably one of the last persons to have seen him. Was she friend or enemy? He had to know.

The plan was foolhardy.

He grimaced. Too late to let the voice of reason interrupt. He darted a quick look at Nina, half lying there with ominous silence hanging between them. He had no doubt she was thinking murder. His impulsive plan could cost him everything.

Crazy last-minute decisions! Fueled by vodka. Damn Kostya. If he had a little warning and some time, he would have approached this a little differently. Maybe. He wasn't sure. He kind of enjoyed carrying her off like that. Maybe he could get her tipsy too.

The plan was foolhardy, dude. You think she's going to cooperate?

He grimaced at his inner voice mocking him. He cussed at his friend again.

Drei owned a small house by Tööstuse, so he didn't have far to go. Luke had kept an eye on it long enough to know no one was monitoring it. Drei had always had his mail directed elsewhere and the area had enough vacation apartments and homes that no one was suspicious of long absences.

The house was dark and not easy to find. When he'd first visited, Luke had pulled down the shades so he could search the place for clues, but several visits had given none. It was a non-descriptive place, normal and unrevealing.

The Paldiski port area was comparably underdeveloped and probably why Drei had chosen the place. Luke circled the street several times before driving down the small driveway. He pulled into the little garage and closed the entrance. His captive didn't move at all when he opened the passenger door. He studied her carefully before unbuckling the belt. One never knew. Razor blades could easily be hidden in those tight clothes and he was sure she was plenty angry with him. Angry enough to hurt him. He also needed to be extra careful since he didn't intend to hurt her.

And how are you going to make an angry operative talk?

He wasn't Drei. He'd never interrogated anyone with covert methods before. It was much easier during his Ranger days.

Unplugging the seat belt, he unwound the loops that held her. "Not far now," he murmured, as he scooped her into his arms.

He'd expected more struggling but she didn't move. Instead, her head cocked at the sounds around her—doors opening, the couple of steps he climbed, the clack of his boots on the wooden floor. The light fixture in the hallway was on automatic timer so he could easily make his way to Drei's room in the back.

He laid her down and felt her stiffen with realization that it was a bed. Yeah, he'd fantasized doing this part with her once or twice, but not under these circumstances. His lips twisted. Probably wouldn't have a chance in the near future either.

"I'm removing the hood," he told her. "The lights are on, so close your eyes."

She blinked several times as her eyes adjusted, looked cursorily around, then turned to glare at him as he removed her gag. She coughed.

"Where am I?" she hissed.

"A bedroom."

"I can see that, Captain Obvious."

He shrugged. "You asked an obvious question."

She stared up at him stonily. "So. You want unobvious questions. What's the speed of scrambled brain? How does a stupid man cross the road? Do you want to die? Oh, wait, strike the third question. It is *obvious* you do."

Luke had suspected a smart mouth on her but he hadn't expected the biting humor. He pulled up a chair, sat down and stretched his legs out. Her eyes narrowed as she studied him from head to toe, no doubt planning pain for his future. He, himself was trying to decide which direction to take with her.

"I needed to talk to you quickly. Setting up a formal meeting with your handlers didn't suit me because that would take time."

Her short laugh didn't sound very helpful. "It isn't the first time you've negotiated for favors, right? This?" She jiggled her captive hands. "Is not conducive to friendly negotiation. This makes me very, very unhelpful."

He hoped being direct and business-like would soothe her. "I just need your help and then you're free to go. I'll owe you a future favor."

Her amusement was palpable now. "That's it? And here I thought you kidnapped me because you couldn't *not* have me any longer. You sure that's all you want?"

She was a cool one, half-lying on that rumpled bed with her hands cuffed, a knowing gleam in her eye. The picture she made was provocative and very tempting. She knew he had the hots for her and was using it to distract him.

Luke understood seduction. Especially the dangerous kind. To hell with being business-like. He stood up and casually unzipped his leather jacket. The intensity of her gaze seared him.

"We've been sending signals for a while now," he said. "I've wanted more, but word is that your agency's strict about mixing pleasure with business, but I'm perfectly willing to overlook that rule if you are."

"That rule is about self-preservation."

Her gaze traveled lower, the heat in her eyes hitting him right between the legs.

"Yours or mine?"

"Both, I suspect."

Luke dropped back into the chair and leaned forward. "You don't strike me as one who follows the rules." He ran one finger down the zipper of her jacket. "Besides, bending the rules is what we do best."

Her voice was a mere whisper. "Are you going to free me before we---negotiate this favor?"

He shook his head. "I'm the one bending the rules here. Answer a few questions and you're free. That way, you can report to your handlers you weren't...willing. Unlike you, I have more leeway in my dealings. When you need my help, just call me."

"What if I kidnap you and tie you up instead?"

He gave her a slow smile. "That would work too."

CHAPTER THREE

Nina couldn't take her eyes off him.

His smile had enough heat to melt the bed. What was that question she threw at him about a scrambled brain? She must have meant hers. Because right now, all she could think was of him on top of her, doing a lot more than questioning.

Seduction was obviously on his mind too. This wasn't going to be easy. He was both charming and infuriating. Sexy and funny too. An irresistible combination.

If she answered his questions, she could find out how he knew her name. It was paramount that her identity remained a secret, especially now, when she was so close to achieving her goals.

"What do you want to know?"

He pulled out folded papers from inside his jacket. He set them in front of her. Photographs of her and—

"Andrei Kamarov," her captor said. "Or sometimes Drei to his friends. You were with him and not long after he disappeared."

Nina lowered her gaze, hoping to hide her shock. Drei Kamarov. Who took those photographs? Drei said to trust no one unless—

"Drei," she drawled, and shrugged. "He was just doing business with me."

Luke flipped over another piece of paper. This time, the picture was of them kissing. "Try again," he said, dryly. "Come on, Naya. Cut the crap and give me something here."

"First, how did you find out my name?" she asked. "Very few people know."

His eyes revealed nothing. "Natalina Litchenko. Twenty seven years old. Daughter of Alexander Litchenko, better known as Spider, an informant who escaped to England after securing the freedom of his wife and daughter to the United States while he stayed under house arrest as part of the agreement. Student at Ohio U, starting an internship at a chicken farm—" He paused, eyebrow raised. "Want me to continue? You don't look well, sweetheart."

Nina felt sick to her stomach. She'd been so careful. Here she'd thought she was unknown, especially in Estonia. They'd assured her, with her having grown up overseas and dyeing her hair black, no one would connect her with her father. It hadn't been good enough, apparently.

"It wasn't a chicken farm internship. It was organic farming." She slumped back against the headboard. "That's a pretty good digger you hired. No one knew the truth, only Drei."

"Were you and he lovers?"

She narrowed her eyes. "Is that part of what you want to know?"

"No."

"So this is just to satisfy your curiosity?"

"I'd rather know before kissing you again."

She arched her eyebrows. "Confident you'll get a second shot, aren't you? Very presumptuous that I'd welcome it."

He leaned forward then, his lips inches from her, his big body covering but not touching hers. "Oh yeah."

"Kiss me again and I'll hurt you."

"Self-preservation not my strongest suit," he murmured, his breath hot against her lips.

She breathed in his scent. This attraction between them was so potent, if he touched her, she was sure the bed was going to combust into flames. She'd resisted for over half a year, keeping her distance, but here, practically in bed, she could feel her rule of no involvement slowly melting away.

Those masculine lips that had given her more fantasies that she'd care to admit were so temptingly near. She wanted to trace their outline with her tongue. The heated moment hung between them, dangerously hot.

"Drei and I are just friends," she finally said. "He was very helpful with certain problems of mine."

"Are those problems connected with your sudden appearance in this part of the world? I mean, you disappeared from a chicken farming internship to—what—play cloak-and-daggers games?"

"Maybe I needed excitement in my life. Maybe chicken farming wasn't my thing."

"Or maybe you needed information you couldn't get unless you're back in the muck, and I don't mean chicken shit."

The man was far too witty for his own good. Who was he to Drei, anyway?

"He's also a friend of mine," he continued, "and I've been looking for him."

So had she, actually. "I haven't seen him since that same meeting in the picture. I suggest you ask the person who gave you those printouts where he or she found the info."

Luke regarded her for a second. His gaze, intense and intimate, made her shift uncomfortably.

"I will," he said. "A meeting? That one picture gives the impression it was a date."

Nina smiled. "It was a date. We had dinner, talked and laughed. Such a nice flirtation." She gazed at him enquiringly. "Surely I'm allowed to date a friend. You're being nosy for no reason."

He frowned. "I do have a reason. You were one of the last people he saw. I'm trying to figure out what he was working on to give me an idea what could have happened to him."

"He could have just gone dark, you know," she pointed out. "Our kind just disappears for a while."

"He'd have left me a message."

Nina looked at him speculatively. Drei had told her he didn't have many friends and if he were to go dark, nobody here would notice. But Luke St. James wasn't from here. Had, in fact, only shown up around these parts *after* Drei's disappearance. Could he be telling the truth?

"Why would he? Is he a good friend of yours?" she asked.

"Yes. He's like a brother to me."

That good a friendship, huh? But still, Drei couldn't have told him about her. But perhaps Luke could be an asset. Her father had taught her, one couldn't sacrifice all one's rooks in a war. She made an offering.

"Drei and I exchange information sometimes," she said. "It's normal for fixers like us to do that."

"But *La Niña* has a reputation of being untouchable," he pointed out, watching her with those incredible eyes.

She shrugged. "It's a reputation. You have one too. Are you really a walking, talking cowboy?"

His answering smile was downright too damn sexy. "I am. Can you tell me what information you two shared?"

Nina frowned. "You're kidding me, right? Like I would tell you."

It was his turn to shrug. "Can't hurt to ask. Drei was looking for information about some political big wig going down—who, time, place, that sort of thing. I thought I'd help him because I have my own sources too."

She kept her expression bland, but her heart skipped a little at what the Cowboy had revealed. No wonder they'd been bumping into each other so much. He'd been seeking the same things too. Political parties, soirees, cryptic messages about some head-of-state. That had been why she and Drei had gotten together. He'd needed to put some puzzle pieces together and she was helping him gather the parts. In return, he'd help get that information to her father through his contacts and perhaps, she'd get to hug her father again instead of talking in code via a computer screen.

"Look," she said. "I can't help you any more because I have no further information. You asked and I answered your questions. I'm kind of looking for Drei myself. I could work harder and check around with some sources of mine, but you'll have to free me. My people will be looking for me soon if I don't make contact."

She needed to get out of here and find out more about Luke St. James. A fixer looking for a missing person was unsurprising, but looking and asking for a missing Drei was sending warning signals in her head. Without her ally, she had to be extra careful.

He looked at her thoughtfully for a second. "All right. I'm taking you back to the car, but you have to put the hood back on. Where do you want to be let off?"

His quick capitulation surprised and, sort of disappointed, her. She couldn't help a parting shot. "That's it? However do you ever get your information? There are so many things you haven't tried yet. I'm surprised you lasted this long in this business."

He gave her one of those dark stares that made her hot all over. His hands hesitated on her cuffs, as if he was reconsidering. Then he smiled, a slow curve of his lips.

"I last as long as needed," he told her, and added, "You're right. I should try something before releasing you."

Something in his tone of voice told Nina he wasn't talking about business.

* * *

Luke knew he should let her go. A missing operative could bring stuff down on his head. The sight of Miss Litchenko cuffed to a bed was giving him images that had nothing to do with getting information. He wanted to take her clothes off piece by piece. He wanted to take off his own clothes and then slide between those long luscious legs. Lots of images of sweaty sheets followed. He smiled.

It must be Kotya's damn vodka. He was usually more reserved. But *La Niña* up close and personal was very potent. Her challenging stare spurred him on.

"Would you like to try the theory out?" His invitation came out before he could stop himself. "I know I would."

She sat very still as he ran his finger on the metal cuff and around her wrist, resting on her pulse. Her heart was racing. He gently massaged the area, his gaze meeting hers. Slowly, he brought her cuffed hand up while he bent down, still looking at her. Her lips opened a fraction. He ran his tongue along the inside of her wrist. Her teeth caught her lower lip. Not taking his eyes off hers, he pushed the sleeve up and licked his way along the soft flesh and nibbled the inside of her elbow. Her head fell back against the pillows, her eyes closed to half-slits. Her sultry expression made already tight places feel even tighter. Hotter.

"Are you going to make me tell you?" she whispered.

"I thought you said you've nothing else to tell," he whispered back, giving her another little nibble.

"If you keep doing that, I'll think of something."

She was temptation personified. He'd wanted her for so long. All these months, he'd wanted and resisted, and now, they were alone together. It looked like the lady wanted him too, unless she was trying to trick him.

Maybe it was time to go a little further.

He reached down and boldly touched the front of her pants. She went very still but didn't voice any protest. Her big, dark eyes, so beautiful and expressive, stared into his challengingly. Not taking his eyes away, he cupped her. Her lower body reared up, pressing against his hand.

"You're in bed, tied up. You're right, I don't think I should pass up the chance to seduce you," he told her.

"Maybe I'm seducing you," she countered, then gasped.

He looked down at her, his hand moving deliberately between her legs. "You think?" He pulled at the zipper in the way. "May I?"

"What if I say no?"

"If you aren't wet down there already, I'll zip your pants back up," he promised. She was undulating against his hand, so he was fairly confident he'd win this bet. He slowly pulled at the zipper, giving her a chance to tell him to stop. When she didn't, he slipped his hand inside. A tight fit there, just like his pants was right now. His triumph was tempered with his need. "So wet, baby."

There was hardly any room to move but the sight of her skinny black thong and all that was revealed sent hot currents of anticipation down his spine. Slowly, gently, he let one finger explore, looking for the right spot. Another small gasp escaped her lips. Found it. He leaned forward over her pliant body, resting one hand on the headboard, so that the tip of his finger could reach lower into her wet heat. Then he drew a long glide upwards and then down again, repeating it a few times. Her eyes closed. The lady was very, very wet.

"Can I take your pants off now?" He teased, feeling both tense and exhilarated at the same time. All his usual caution had long flown out the proverbial window. "If you don't come in the next five minutes, I'll put them back on."

Her eyes flickered open. She made to say something and he slid his finger inside her, interrupting whatever she had in mind. Instead, a half-formed word came out and her neck arched up. He wanted to nibble there too, but first things first. He didn't let up, making circles with his thumb as he pushed his finger deeper into that incredibly tight heat. God, he wanted to push something else inside her.

He'd never been one to wait too long to pick up his advantage. His rodeo experience came in handy again. He could pull at and fold limbs and legs, and in mere seconds, do whatever needed to get his quarry. Jerking her pants down and off with her soft black shoes was easy. Pulling her legs apart and over his shoulders took only a second. Damp pink flesh, beckoning for a taste. The scent of female desire hit his nostrils. He went a little crazy. Placing his mouth where he wanted, he worked his tongue over her clitoris, making sure to stroke it the same way his finger had been. Savoring her with his tongue. Kissing her deeply.

This time there was room to slide in two fingers as he lapped at Nina's clit, working that wetness to his advantage, finding sensitive nerve endings until her moans told him she was close. Her squirming body froze as she neared her orgasm and he pressed down firmly with tongue and fingers. The taste of her filled his mouth as she came, sexy whimpers coming from her throat.

Not letting up, he moved up from between her thighs and climbed over her, giving her a hard kiss on her mouth.

"Can I take off my pants now?" He murmured against her lips, moving her cuffed hands over his bulge. "Can I fuck you? I promise if you don't like it, I'll stop and put my pants back on."

"Did you take me prisoner...to...only make promises and ask dumb questions?"

He smiled at her husky sassiness. "But you're answering them so well, being tied up and all. When my prisoner gives me what I want, I reward them. Do you want your reward now?"

Her answer was her hand clenching on the front of his pants, squeezing non-too-lightly. "Show me this reward," she invited.

* * *

Nina's heart raced as she watched the pair of male hands slowly unbuttoning his fly. Apparently, the wild and loud thumping she kept hearing in her head had knocked her brain senseless.

She was supposed to be pissed-off. She should be lying any way she could to get herself out of here. She should be planning ways to make this man pay for taking her prisoner. So many 'shoulds' that were taking their places way down the list of 'important things to do immediately.'

The Cowboy was seducing her and she was allowing it to happen. Okay, that was a laughable choice of word. Allowing? She was tied up and enjoying the whole thing. His fingers, his tongue—holy cow, that tongue. Had all these months of built-up sexual tension between them paid off. One intimate kiss from him and she had the best orgasm she could remember. And she didn't want him to stop.

He shucked his pants off, underwear and all. She stared at his erection.

No, she definitely didn't want him to stop. She cleared her throat as she watched him take a few moments to quickly sheathe a condom.

"I can't wait, sweetheart. I want to be inside you right now."

She wanted to have him inside her too. In fact, she badly wanted to hold that beautiful penis in her hands and do her own exploration.

He was on top of her before she could take another look, and she gasped at the intimate contact between her legs. Nothing tentative about this man at all. In her current world of constant negotiations and deliberate counter moves, she liked how he did things. So damn American.

Her breath came out in a soft gush as he pushed against her tender and willing flesh. Her legs parted on their own to accommodate him. He felt big and hot, the long slow stroke as he entered her rubbed already sensitive nerves, making her shiver. His face was close to hers and he stared into her eyes as he slowly and surely entered her inch by hard inch.

He was all the way in her now. Then he started grinding against her with tiny strokes, rocking against her clitoris. The sensation was deliciously tortuous.

"So can I start interrogating you now?" he asked, his voice a husky murmur.

She laughed as the heat down there escalated. He was so deliciously evil too.

"You think I'd capitulate so easily?"

He rocked harder and she bit down on her lower lip to stop from moaning.

"I count on your resistance," he told her. "This interrogation could go on for hours and hours. We barely have our clothes off. I'll make you come again and again until you give me what I want."

Hours and hours?

She sighed. "I don't have hours and hours and you know it. Besides, you're contradicting yourself. We agreed this was a reward, not an interrogation."

"Oh. Well, thanks for reminding me," he said, starting moving in and out of her in long, sure strokes.

* * *

Her hips matched his, stroke for stroke.

Luke found his eyes closing. The feel of her was incredible. Slick heat. Glove-tight. He wished he wasn't wearing protection so he could feel how wet she was. He wished he'd taken the time to undress all of her instead of being in such a male hurry. Maybe next—

Her feminine purrs of approval urged him on as her cuffed hands between their bodies clawed at his shirt front. He heard buttons popping. He felt her tightening around his hard length, pulling at him, milking him, hurrying him on even though he wanted to slow down a bit and savor her. There was a buzz starting in the back of his neck and a fuse was lighting its way from there all the way down his spine to the tip of his cock. He could feel that fire burning, making its way to an orgasmic explosion. Her urgent hands scratching his chest demanded less finesse. Taking a deep breath, he pushed into her fiercely—

The backfire of a motorcycle outside the window brought their frenzy to an immediate stop, like hitting pause in a movie, their eyes wide and alert, their whole bodies clenched in mid-action. The sensuous haze in his head screamed in frustrated need and he could feel his lower back muscles clenching and unclenching, wanting to keep pushing into that sweet heat.

More noise outside the window.

Luke cursed quietly. He moved quickly, ignoring his body and mind protesting as he pulled out of the gorgeous, hot woman beneath him.

"Maybe it's a passing vehicle," Nina whispered.

He shook his head. "Drei's place has a long driveway. That was from right outside the house."

Her eyes widened. "We're in Drei's house."

Ah, well. So much for secrecy. He nodded as he quickly unlocked her cuffs. "I don't know who's down there but I have a feeling, at this late hour, they aren't friends."

"Maybe it's Drei."

She got out of the bed. Lucas sighed at the luscious pair of long legs begging for his attention.

"If it is, he's got lousy timing," he muttered.

She followed the direction of his gaze, then transferred her sultry stare toward him deliberately. "Agreed," she said softly.

He wanted to laugh. They were both half-naked, still turned on from their interrupted lovemaking, and trying very hard to focus on a possible threat. He cocked his head, taking note of the telltale sounds of three creaky steps Drei had warned him about. Correction. Not Drei. Not one, but multiple threats.

CHAPTER FOUR

"What is it?" Nina picked up her pants, quickly turning them right-side-out.

His gaze had turned watchful. He'd pulled on his pants and was quickly buttoning up his fly with one hand while his other played with his cell phone. His expression hardened.

"What?" she asked again as she walked."

"Do you know these people?" Luke showed her the shadowy images on his phone.

Luke had obviously installed cameras outside Drei's house that connected wirelessly to his smartphone. They were blurry shadows. She shook her head.

"Time to go then," Luke decided.

"But what if they're friends of Drei?" She asked.

"Creeping about with hand signals. Sure. You staying to find out?"

Nina combed her hair off her face. "No need to be so sarcastic. I think you not getting your reward has made you grouchy, Cowboy."

He gave a quiet laugh. "Their timing sucks."

She couldn't agree more. She didn't resist when he pulled her in to give her a hard kiss.

"What's the plan? It's your call since you're obviously familiar with the upstairs of Drei's house." She looked around. "I hope this isn't his room. We've made a mess."

"Wait, are you saying you're familiar with Drei's downstairs?"

She grinned. "Knew you'd catch that. You want to talk now when—" She gestured to the window. "—some bad guys are coming in to rob Drei? I wonder what he has in here."

That was the only reason she could come up with why there were men heading up Drei's house this late. They couldn't be after her since being here hadn't been her plan, therefore, they must be after Drei or Cowboy.

Luke shook his head. "Nothing. I've searched every nook and cranny. Drei's place is clean. Not a clue."

But what was he looking for? She didn't have time to ask as she peered over his shoulder again. "They have night goggles on too," she noted in a low voice. "And those glints in the moonlight aren't from their wristwatches."

"We'll have to leave the car and go out the back window."

"If I remember, the river's in the back. I don't swim. Now what?"

He sighed. "Come on."

There was no choice but to follow him. He opened the back window and it made a sliding noise as he did so. The chilly air wafted in. He shrugged at her and ducked his head outside into the dark. Then his big body followed in one graceful glide. A hand appeared, offering help.

Nina rolled her eyes and pushed it away. As if she needed a hand to climb out of a window!

It took a few seconds to adjust her eyes to the darkness. The light from the room streamed out, showing the slope of the roof and shadows and angles of tree branches.

He grabbed her hand and pulled her along behind him and she had to concentrate on keeping up with his bigger strides. She wondered whether she'd first get hurt from being shot at or from falling off a roof as they scrambled down the slope to the edge.

"Wait," he ordered softly.

Like she had anywhere else to go at the edge? She swallowed a gasp when he released her hand and simply jumped off, disappearing over the side of the roof. She peered over. The man? Insane. The jump? Kind of hot.

"Jump." His whisper traveled up to her.

"You're kidding, right?"

"Naya, jump. I've got you."

She stood there looking down at his shadow. If he missed.... She looked behind her. Looked back down at Luke's shadow.

"Jump," he said, again. "Don't fall forward. Don't fling yourself. Pretend you're stepping off the pool into water. I've got you."

She did as he ordered, taking care not to jump on top of him. There was a second of breathless weightlessness and then strong arms gathered around her thighs, sliding up her back as she fought for balance. She put her hands onto his shoulders. In the dark, she felt them shake with amusement even as she realized his face was buried intimately against the front of her jeans. Slowly, he slid her body down, not breaking the close contact.

"I prefer doing that without clothes," he whispered. "Next time, the top comes off too."

She pushed against him. "There might not be a next time," she muttered.

"Let's be positive," he said, pulling her along.

"What next?"

"Drei has a bike in the shed at the back. Don't worry, I've ridden it."

Yes, she remembered Drei's motorcycle, a powerful hulk of noisy proportions. They were probably going to get killed but the hand holding hers was insistent and she followed him down the short path. They reached the small shed and behind her, she heard some voices shouting.

"I see them! Back there!"

Luke pushed open the door and they ran inside. He seemed familiar with the place, going to the right. She stumbled along behind him, marveling at his lithe quickness as he climbed onto the dark machine. It was running in one smooth turn of the key.

"Jump behind me," he ordered.

She did so.

"Hang on tight. It's going to be a cattle chase."

"What?"

"Just a lot of circling around while we try to get on the road. Just keep your head down. It all depends on whether they decide to shoot or chase us with their bikes."

Great. This was all she needed to hear, that she might be shot at while riding as a passenger. Time was running out and she hadn't the time to change her mind.

"Where did you put my gun?" she asked. If she was going down in a hail of bullets, she wasn't going out without a fight.

The bike took off. There were shouts as they emerged out of the shed.

"In the front of my jacket," he replied, shouting over the ensuing noise of bikes and shouts.

Nina put her arms around Luke, slid one inside his jacket and found his holster immediately. She wished she had more time to explore. The man felt hard and...

The motorcycle roared as they went down the pathway, swerving left, then right. The wind and engine noise masked a lot of the other commotion but she caught sight of other headlights coming on. Their house invaders had decided to pursue.

The path was bumpy and Nina found herself automatically fisting Luke's belt. His head turned.

"Hang on tight," he yelled, and sped up just as the sound of gunshots rang.

Their bike raced past one car and several bikes, zigzagging, circling, raising clumps of dirt and grass and spitting them every direction. Nina gasped as somehow they flew through the air, hit the hood of the car and continued riding over the top and down the back. Her backside went up and down as if she were riding rodeo. Cowboy was definitely doing his thing. She fired off several shots, causing the other bikes to swerve away.

"Good girl!" Luke yelled.

She didn't have time to yell back because they were flying in the air again, this time a good ten or more feet. She hung on for dear life as they came back down in a crash, tearing a hole in the earth. She had no idea how Luke managed to land on two wheels and how they were still speeding away. Somehow, in all her preparations through the years to be a fixer, she'd not envisioned she would be doing extreme biking in Estonia. In the dark. With people shooting at her.

She laughed. Exhilaration coursed through her like a current. Damn, but this was the kind of fun she liked. Nothing stealthy and all action. She turned and started shooting at the headlights, emptying her cartridge. Tires screeched and the headlights swerved erratically. She was on target with a couple of shots, as the headlights went dark. Take that, unknown armed enemies!

"I need more ammo," she yelled into Luke's ear as they entered the street.

"There's another cartridge in the inside pocket," he yelled back.

Nina reached around and slipped her hand inside the other side of his jacket. The bumpy ride made it an interesting experience. She finally found the pocket.

Load, turn, fire.

One of the bikes following them skidded.

"Any more weapons if I run out?"

"One more, baby. It's waiting for you."

She put her hand in one of his pockets. "Where is it?"

"Lower."

"Not that one!"

His masculine laughter was sexy, even over the racket. He handled the big machine with expert ease, as if he'd ridden with reckless abandon a lot in his life. Part of her thrilled to his mastery, fascinated by his calm at being chased and shot at. He sped the bike around bends and over slopes, weaving between a few cars which were out late, dodging their chasers in hair-raising ways. Hanging on tightly, she vaguely noted he was heading straight toward the city lights.

"Won't that bring out the police?" she asked.

"Exactly. Maybe they'd stop shooting so much. I can handle them chasing us, but would prefer not to do so with holes in either one of us."

She agreed. Sure enough, as soon as the thugs realized the direction Luke was taking the bike, the number of shots began to dwindle.

"It seems our pursuers don't want the authorities involved," Luke said.

"They're right behind us, though. Where are we going?"

"How many bikes still behind us?"

"Only one. I took one down and another must have crashed when it swerved."

"Good. I'm taking us down one of the alleys and then it'll just be that bike behind us. Once I take care of that, we'll have to find a way out of that alley because you know the other cars will be waiting at either end."

He didn't wait for her acquiescence, racing the bike down the road at a dangerous speed. She hung onto his belt precariously, as she turned to check behind her. They were speeding up too.

Luke handled the bike like a pro, passing cars and bouncing back and forth from the cobblestone pavement to road and back again. Lamp posts whizzed by at heart-jarring flashes. She tried not to think about how close they were.

"Here we are. Hang on!" Luke warned and then the bike was mid-air over some parked cars and back down on its wheels. When they miraculously landed upright, he yelled to her, "Are you okay?"

"My butt hurts from all that bouncing," she replied facetiously.

He laughed, which wasn't the usual thing people getting shot at do. Maybe he thought he was in one of those old cowboy movies, where shootouts were the regular thing. She could only hang on as this crazy, delicious man did stunts that made her squeeze her eyes tightly shut, sliding in between moving vehicles and finally, gunning for a dark alley as their pursuers avoided accidents.

"There is a small smoke explosive in the inside left pocket of my jacket," he instructed while their bike roared toward the alley. "Just pull the top and throw it behind us. It'll get the motorcycle. That will leave just the two cars."

She found it immediately and as they zoomed down the long and narrow path, she looked back at the pursuing bike. She pulled the small cap and tossed the explosive at them. She didn't hear anything because of the roar of the bikes reverberating against the old brick and stone walls, but billowing smoke began to rapidly rise like a ghostly apparition in a movie, enveloping the pursuing bike, effectively blinding the driver and his passenger. As they moved further down, she heard the unmistakable crash of a bike meeting a wall.

"Good," Luke said, slowing down the bike. "The others have to get out of their cars to come in after us. We have options."

"Options?" All she could think of was escape.

"Stay and fight them and find out who they are. Run and find out who they are ourselves. Get a room and fuck and not care who they are."

Naya jumped off the bike when it came to a stop. "You're crazy!" she announced. "They're after you, so why do I care who they are?"

"Oh good, then we'll just go straight to the third option. Your place or mine?"

She wanted to scream and kick at him. "If we weren't about to get shot, I'd shoot you myself," she declared. "Do you have an escape route with this brilliant idea of holing up in a dark alley or do I have to fucking save your ass?"

* * *

Luke laughed softly. He hadn't felt this alive in months. Imminent danger around the corner. Death threatening at his doorstep. The familiar exhilaration of facing near-impossible odds. Hell, yeah. He missed his Ranger days out in the field—running, chasing, hiding, moving, and attacking everything going at breakneck speed, with every decision being made at rapid fire. He missed his days ranching and chasing wild horses too. Life that was on the move, not like this past year, where everything was a constant test of his patience.

The woman with him made him feel alive too. She was fearless, funny and sexy as hell. Kidnapping, gunfire, car chases, going Evel Knievel on a motorcycle and more hadn't phased her one bit. She was spitting mad and taking him on.

God, he wanted to just do her against the wall right now.

He was well aware that he was acting out of character. Hell, this whole night had been crazy. He'd finally gotten one big lead to his brother and what did he do? Let his dick do the talking, that was what.

No more talking. Every time he tried, his dick interrupted and he lost concentration.

Grabbing Nina by the hand, he pulled her down further into a side alley. She followed without further questions, moving with that nimble grace he'd found so damn sexy, whether clad in tight pants or clingy gowns. Okay, maybe one more zinger to get her worked up.

"We'll have to practice in bed once we get rid of these fuckers. Come on!"

Her expletive was very inventive. He grinned. He liked inventiveness in a woman.

"I hear police sirens," she said.

He'd hoped that would happen. He'd chosen this part of town because it was just outside a popular tourist district, with some big name hotels. The authorities would want to check out any reports of a speeding vehicles and flying bullets.

"Good. They might not shoot so indiscriminately."

"Do you even know where you're going?"

"Trust me." He was familiar with a few back streets here, having worked a contract that required looking for a missing weapon in a dumpster. He heard her snort behind him. "Just ahead is a building with a fire escape. If we climb up to the fifth floor the apartment there is registered to someone I know. We can take the stairs to the front side where the parking lot is, and take off from there. I'll drop you off at your place."

"Right, and have them chasing us all over again. No thanks. We part ways once we make it out of this stupid chase."

"If you haven't noticed, I'm pretty good at evasion," Luke pointed out. His experience as a Ranger had returned handily. Old habits, it seemed, didn't go away. His instinct was busy knocking, insisting he was missing a clue. Everything about this chase felt wrong, especially the part where they just showed up after all these months of him going to Drei's place alone, but there wasn't time to talk about this. He'd just have to do things his way. Arguing with the lady would take away more time. Aloud, he added, "But if you insist, we'll split up once we shed those goons. Come on."

His words must have placated her. She followed him with no further argument. They made their way in the dark behind some lowered awnings. He could hear the running footsteps behind them, scrambling about, looking for them. It was just a matter of time before they came by the awnings and started checking behind them.

"We're getting on that balcony," he said, pointing up. "You come up after me and I'll pull you the rest of the way."

"Okay," she said.

After testing the strength of a chain holding back some aluminum panels, he climbed up, then hauled himself over the railing. He looked over. Nina was already climbing up the chain, using the pillar nearby for foot holds. He muscled the chain up, hand over hand, to speed her ascent, then he leaned over the balcony and helped her the rest of the way. She stepped off the chain, balanced on the railing, and when he gave one last tug, she fell against his body. His arm held on to her tightly, while he walked backward, pulling the rest of the chain up so that it wouldn't tumble down with a telltale swing. She had a way of being in sync with him. Wrapping her legs tightly around his waist, she twisted so she could use both her hands to get the chain up quickly.

Not a moment too soon too, since flashlights started marching through the shadows, their paths crisscrossing as their anonymous pursuers continued searching for them. Luke stood very still, one hand around Nina, the two of them hanging on to the chain so it wouldn't clatter. He could feel her warm breath against his cheek, and smell the soft sweet scent she had on.

Damn if he didn't want to kiss her right then. And, much to his surprise, her mouth found his. In the dark, danger lurking beneath them, with his feet planted apart in precarious balance and knowing exactly where her crotch was nesting right against, he found himself responding with quiet ease. Nina ran her tongue lightly against his, sensuously retreating, daring him to come after her. Damn if she wasn't a wicked tease.

The beam from one of the flashlights hit an aluminum panel, momentarily giving the darkness a reflective glow. If the arc of the light changed slightly and if their pursuer looked up, Luke knew he would see their tangled bodies. He held his breath, the corner of his eye, following the small spot of light as it traveled further away. The only thing moving was the soft caress of her tongue and the blood surging between his legs

When the light disappeared around the corner, his tormenter took her lips off his. He licked his, still savoring her taste.

"Good thing we're both clad in black," she whispered.

"Not your panties. It was a deep blue," he reminded her softly as they both quietly dropped the weight of the chain. He slowly lowered her to her feet, her lower body rubbing his intimately. "Piece of lace barely covering some tasty..."

"Shhh," she shushed. "You're going to make me laugh and get us caught. Is this the right building?"

Luke reluctantly let her go. "Next door, actually. It has a fire escape, unlike this one." He took her hand and placed it on the railing. "Follow this to the end. There's a ledge there we can easily jump over."

"Okay."

It was interesting having her beside him. Usually, when they'd met during their jobs, like the first time crawling in tight spaces, they were on opposite sides, doing their thing, so he hadn't had the opportunity to study her. Now, he enjoyed her professional ease at treading in the dark and the fearless, unhurried way she walked on the ledge, even though it was the first time she'd encountered it. Having the perfect partner in any operation was hard to find. In the army, it took years of training with that person or a group of people to be totally familiar with working together as one unit, but he found it was strangely so with Nina. All in one night. He was damned intrigued by this discovery.

They made it over the balcony and up the fire escape without any incidence. He carefully retrieved the apartment key hidden near the windowsill and unlocked the door.

"Where's the owner?" Nina asked, after she came inside.

"Don't know. Don't care. It's empty for now and that's all I care about." He turned on a hallway light.

She glanced around, then gave him a curious look. "What if there's someone here?"

The place was owned by a client on the run for a while who had given him access because of a favor, but Luke wasn't explaining that. "Then, I might have a whole other set of problems on my hands," he replied, lightly. He walked to the front side of the apartment. "This place was chosen because of its easy front and back exits, so make your own brilliant deductions while I check out the window."

The outside looked clear. He knew the cars after them were probably parked on either side of the alleyway they'd entered to block any escape. The police lights were a good deterrent to them making any more gunshots. Hell, they might even be gone, if they were trying to avoid catching attention. Traffic was light, so a quick getaway with no one gunning for them was eminently possible.

He glanced back and found Nina lounging on the sofa, reading a magazine.

"Catching up on your TV shows?" he mocked.

She looked up with a bored expression. "Oh, are you done? Are we safe from your enemies? Can we leave now?"

He cocked his head. "What about all that kissing we were doing just now?"

He was beginning to enjoy teasing her too much, just to watch that warm flush of color blooming across her cheeks. She mostly kept her cool, though, which made it all more fun.

"Oh, that." She yawned. "I figured I needed to shut you up so the bad guys can't hear your incessant yammering. Kissing cured that."

"What about the crotch-nudging? My cock wasn't yammering until you started teasing it." Actually, his cock had been complaining a lot where the lady was concerned. "Now you've got him all hot and bothered and eager for you to kiss him."

"I wasn't crotch...nudging!" She jumped off the couch. "And I'm not kissing him until you get us out of this. I need to report back to my people. I checked my phone and there have been no messages since the last one at Drei's place. You know, the one I ignored because I was tied up?"

"Huh. Let's focus back on the earlier part." Luke made a rewinding gesture with his finger. "You said you aren't kissing my dick until I get us out of this. So, you *are* kissing him later?"

He cocked a brow at the mutinous set of her mouth. Hey, *La Niña* was supposed to be the ice princess of all ice princesses. He was just too delighted to find out what a lie that was. She was molten lava, hot like an enraged volcano, and he couldn't help but keep wanting her to explode all over him. Preferably with both of them naked this time.

"Luke, I'm just about ready to go outside and scream for help so the police will come arrest you for false imprisonment."

"Oh, all right," he said. "Come on, let's get to the parking lot and I'll give you the keys to the car."

She frowned. "What about you?"

"I'll get back to my place, don't worry. This way, you'll have an excuse to come give me the car back and then we can...ah...talk more about any helpful stuff you find out for me."

She narrowed her eyes for a moment, especially at the part where he paused teasingly. "Fine. I'm really late. Let's go."

They made it to the parking lot with no other problem and Luke reluctantly watched her drive away. Then, after she turned a corner, he jumped into a second vehicle and followed her. This way, he would make sure she was safe. He really didn't believe all that happened tonight was 100 percent about him.

* * *

Nina couldn't begin to put into words her jumbled emotions. What the hell happened tonight? Didn't she say to herself it was going to be a quick and easy night because the job was simple? Boy, was that the understatement of the year.

She pursed her lips, trying to decide what to tell her handlers when they debriefed her. She had broken an important protocol by either not sending a message or replying to their communications. They had to assume she'd been compromised. Texting or calling back right now would just generate more questions and she needed time to get her head back in the game.

Cowboy fucked her tonight.

Oh, boy, that wasn't a good place to start to get herself back in control. That man she had been so attracted to all these months had kidnapped her, threatened her and then made her come with his mouth.

50

His beautiful, sexy, Oh-so-talented mouth. And she had actually encouraged him because she couldn't help herself. She couldn't stay angry at him. In fact, she wanted to be naked with him and spend the rest of the night exploring him as much as he'd enjoyed exploring her.

Dammit. Stop thinking about that. Dwell on the important stuff.

Like the fact she'd dropped her façade and basically all but admitted to him her real name was Naya. Plus, she still needed to find out his relationship with Drei and why he was looking for him. Most important of all, her handlers couldn't be told the truth. They would look closely at Drei and she would truly be compromised then.

Damn that stupid, sexy, crazy, sexy, reckless, sexy American! She sighed. As she'd known, he'd complicate her life. She didn't have time for complications. Not now, when she was so close to accomplishing what she'd set out to do. Sexy. She let out an exasperated breath. She couldn't get that dratted man out of her thoughts.

Of course she had to see him again. She needed to find out more about him and Drei because Drei had gone missing for too long. Why had there been a whole gang of people after Luke at Drei's place? They weren't waiting for him to show up because then they would have attacked them the moment Luke arrived with her in tow. She frowned. So, did they just show up when they somehow found out about Drei's house? She remembered Drei's place was quite hidden, with a long driveway, and that was how they had made a mistake by not slowing down quick enough. The sudden backfiring of one of those bikes had alerted Luke and her.

Her mind raced at the implication. Those attackers weren't sure of where they were going. So were they after Luke or Drei? Maybe they'd thought Luke was Drei.

It was a short drive to where she usually received her instructions and debriefed. The location was typical of a black ops facility, in a business district, inside a bland-looking building, surrounded by offices. This one was particularly low-key, acting as some kind of delivery service, which, of course, was partly true, since she was a courier of sorts.

Usually, this late at night, she would go through the secured gates into the underground garage, but the car wasn't hers and she didn't want them to screen it. So she parked a street away instead. The walk gave her a bit of time to come up with a plausible explanation for her handlers. She would stay close to the truth, tell them about being chased by unknown assailants and had to play hide-and-seek until she was no longer followed. She would just leave the parts with Luke out of the story. They wouldn't be happy to know she'd had sex with The Cowboy because the past year, he'd shown up at so many places she'd gone to, looking for almost the same things. Coincidence? She couldn't tell.

So many questions about that man and all she knew for sure was how big his penis was.

She almost giggled out loud at the unexpected observation. Damn it. It had been one hell of a rollercoaster night with her going through a whole gamut of emotions, from anger to arousal to the pure adrenaline of being in danger. And all she could tell was how big The Cowboy's dick was.

She entered the code at the side door. The desk, usually manned, was empty. She frowned. All the TV screens were on but the place was eerily quiet.

Something caught her eye. Blood on the wall, splattered in an unmistakable pattern. She ran over to the desk.

There, behind the overturned chair, was Tomas. She didn't have to walk around to check whether he was dead; part of his head was missing. The silence in the place had turned ominous.

She turned her head and stared in shocked disbelief at the wall of TV screens. Bodies on the screens. Her handlers. A few other operatives. The guards. All dead.

Nina picked up a gun lying on the floor. She realized now she would have been dead if she'd come back early. It hadn't been Luke those men were after. It was her.

* * *

Luke kept a safe distance from Nina. He'd activated the GPS he'd tagged her car with before she'd gotten in, thus it was just a matter of following the signal. He wasn't going to chance her knowing he was following her yet again.

He just wanted to make sure she was safe. Now that he had time alone, away from the delectable *La Niña*, he could actually try to figure out this strange business with the attempt on their lives.

All these months, Drei's place had never been invaded. In fact, he would bet money those guys tonight hadn't even cased the place before. The way they'd driven down to the house indicated they were unsure of where the driveway would lead them. Drei had chosen the residence precisely for that paved driveway. It looked like a regular turn-off until the sharp angle before reaching the house. Those who were unfamiliar with it usually assumed it was part of a road, and the sharp turn and bump down caused one to brake as paved road turned part gravel. That was what had caught his attention and interrupted him and Nina.

His grip on the steering wheel tightened. God. Was he frustrated when they showed up. Nina had been making the sexiest moans, driving him nuts as he thrust into her wet heat. He was still frustrated. Getting side-tracked here, son.

He pushed away the teasing memory of Nina's bared assets. Back to the shooters. He drove by Nina, who was on foot. Ha, the woman was trying to keep his car out of sight so she wouldn't have to explain about him. He couldn't help but smile about that.

He parked in a spot behind another vehicle. It was close enough to keep an eye on Nina, watching her as she disappeared through a side door. A delivery service front. Interesting. Should he stay and wait for her to come out? She would be in there for hours and perhaps leave with someone.

He debated about his next step, half-amused at his worry over a woman who was perfectly capable of taking care of herself. He didn't understand his concern at all, only that slight niggle that something was wrong kept spurring him to ignore common sense.

After all, besides the point about Drei's house tonight, he had been very sure no one had followed them to Drei's place. So how—

That point evaporated when four figures walked past his car and headed straight to the side of the building where Nina had gone into. Luke reloaded his weapons and turn to retrieve a back pack from the backseat. His suspicions weren't baseless after all.

CHAPTER FIVE

Nina ran down the hallway and entered the main office. Pausing at the doorway, she swallowed hard as she surveyed the carnage around her. Her acquaintances—people with whom she'd worked with—lay scattered about the room, the positions of their bodies showing they'd been caught by surprise. Whoever had come in had access to the door codes and had used silencers on the guards in the outside foyer. They had bypassed a few rooms and headed for this one, as if they'd known where their targets were.

She studied the room quickly as she walked past the bodies. Except for the dead, nothing else seemed amiss. The laptops were still running. Everything on the shelves looked untouched. What were they after? She reached the inner office and stopped again at the sight of her handler's assistant, Ana. She was lying on the floor just past the door, as if she'd rushed out and then was immediately shot down. She could tell they were fired at close range, which meant the assailants had already reached the door by the time Ana came out.

Carefully, she stepped over the body. In comparison with the other rooms, this one was a mess. File cabinets were opened, their contents pulled or thrown out. Desk drawers, boxes, shelves, files—nothing was left untouched, it seemed. They must have been here for a bit of time looking for...for what?

She didn't have to check her handler's slumped body to know he was dead. Blood was splattered all down the back of his head and shoulders. Hendrik had been shot from behind, so his killer had been standing there.

Her eyes widened. A photo of hers was on her handler's computer screen. She took a deep breath and walked slowly toward the desk. The smell of blood was getting to her and she had to swallow several times. It was even worse when she finally stood behind Hendrik and saw the hole in the back of his head.

Don't think about it. Look at the screen. Read!

It was her personnel file—name, age, that sort of thing. Nothing especially notable. She clicked the backward key on the keyboard. The screen changed to show all her login times. She hadn't done so all night at that point, of course. It was then she noticed the cell phone still in Hendrik's hand by the keyboard. Peering forward, she tapped on it to turn it on.

Nina frowned. It was the text to her. Why was her handler texting her while checking her login time? Of course, she hadn't answered his last one, but still, he would know exactly when she was last in here. Unless...unless it was the killers seeking information about her, which would mean—

The blinking light above the office exit alerted her that someone was entering. Hendrik would usually look up at the small TV above it to see who was coming in or out, except this time, it was just a blank screen. Someone was in the place, though, and she had a bad feeling they were here looking for her, as they had been all night.

She readied her weapon.

* * *

Luke ran across the street. The men, the glint of their weapons visible in the shadows, were already keying in the code to get inside, which told him one of them was either the insider or knew someone from the inside.

No way could this bunch be part of Nina's organization. Apart from the weapons in their hands, fixers were also notorious loners and seldom traveled in a pack. This group smelled of something familiar and deadly. The way they assembled, filed in, and held their weapons. The silent way they communicated. The kick into action without pause. It all reminded him of a covert team assassination.

Luke knew he only had a slight advantage. They didn't know he was out here, behind them.

As they slipped in through the metal door, Luke reached the opening just in time to toss in his weapon of choice in such a situation. Then he lightly closed the door and dropped to the ground, rolling several feet away. On his stomach, he pointed his weapon at the door and waited.

"Sorry, Nina, babe," he muttered. Under the circumstances, this was the best he could do.

He mentally counted. A smoke grenade detonated immediately, enveloping the blast-area in smoke. The effect of his homemade one would give some respiratory problems, especially at close range. He was counting on that. They should be rushing out soon. His fingers were crossed that Nina and her friends inside would take out their surprised visitors and wouldn't be too surprised themselves. He wasn't going to wait too long, though.

"Let's see who's smart enough to run back out here instead of toughing it out in there." He waited grimly. A direct kill hadn't been his thing for a while.

* * *

Nina risked a peek through the blinds. She dismissed the idea of waiting in here for the intruders. The prospect of not being found in this dead-end room was nigh impossible. Perhaps if she moved out and hid somewhere, she might trick them into believing she wasn't here. It was quite clear to her what they were back for. For some reason, they were looking for her.

She took a deep breath, opened the door and carefully peered out. She could hear sounds coming from the front. There was a loud clatter and muffled voices followed. She stepped out of the room and headed for the door that connected to the main passageway.

The strange noises continued, some sort of scuffling and a few shouts. Nina frowned. How strange. It sounded like a bunch of bodies wrestling on the ground out there.

Keeping her weapon ready for any surprises, she turned the door handle and opened it a few inches.

Her frown deepened. Coughing and gasping? She opened the door a few inches wider. The distinct smell of smoke wafted in. She sniffed the air, catching a familiar odor. More coughing came from the direction of the foyer. It was hazy and getting harder to see. Almost immediately, a dark figure rushed in her direction and the glass window next to her shattered.

Nina pulled the trigger. The man fell in a loud thud a few feet away. He had on dark clothing. A face mask obscured his features. The smoke was getting thicker. Was there a fire? What the fucking hell was going on?

* * *

Luke waited with deadly calm. Two of the dark-clothed men rushed out of the door, one firing his weapon in several directions. Like his, the man's gun was equipped with a silencer, so no loud shots rang out. Several thuds hit the ground near Luke, raising dirt and dust like killer raindrops.

He didn't hesitate. He took both out with two shots. He eyed the smoke coming out of the door. Come on. Two more.

Then he heard one distinct shot. No silencer. He ran to the entrance. A second shot fired.

Only two? Surely Nina's people would be mowing these men down like nobody's business. Where was everybody?

"Nina?" Luke yelled out.

A familiar figure stepped out of the smoke. A neckerchief was tied around her face like a cowboy. She pulled it off and wheezed a little. His relief at finding her safe was palpable. Those shots—

"Did you get any of them?" he asked quickly.

"Two. Another smoke grenade, Cowboy? Where the hell do you keep getting them?"

Luke exhaled. "In my special cowboy backpack, of course."

58

"How sexy."

She was the coolest female he'd ever come across. A keeper. He hauled her into his arms and kissed her possessively.

CHAPTER SIX

Kissing him was fast becoming an addiction. Nina wanted so much more. She didn't say anything as he practically commandeered her away from the place back to his car. Then she carefully pulled off the laptop she'd hurriedly strapped on. She had wrapped bubble wrap and a belt around it and slung it across her back like a bow to keep her hands free. She glanced out the window, wondering where Luke was taking her to now.

Note to self. Must teach this man to ask first, then carry her off. Really, he should just change his name from Cowboy to Caveman, the way he kept taking off with her so damn possessively.

Mmmm. Her stomach clenched at the image of Luke taking her possessively. She had it bad.

"We need to talk," Luke said, as he drove off.

"Oh, talking," she said dismissively. "Questions again? How about, how many freaking cars do you own? Why were you following me again? And yeah, the most important one—those guys...were they after you or after me? Because it suddenly looked like it was me those same bastards were trying to kill."

Those intense green eyes slanted at her briefly. "They showed up at Drei's place at a weird hour to catch someone by surprise. Since my decision to go there was...spur of the moment...I had a suspicion all along that it was you, babe." He smiled slowly at the narrow-eyed look she was giving him. "I really didn't mean to kidnap you. Things happened unexpectedly."

"That about sums up tonight," she pointed out in a dry voice. She gave him a quick rundown of what she'd seen inside and continued, "It still started with you. I've been thinking, too. If you hadn't interrupted me tonight, I'd have gone straight back to meet with my people and might have..."

She shrugged, unable to finish. Those people were mostly her acquaintances but she'd known them for long enough to have shared some jokes and even gone out to dinner and drinks on occasion. She would have been sitting in Hendrik's office when the shooters came. She might have run out behind him to see what was happening too and lying on the floor right now.

"I'm sorry about your friends."

She shrugged again and looked down at her hands on her lap. "I wouldn't call them friends. Because of our jobs, we hardly know anything intimate about each other. But the sight of them like that...."

Again, she couldn't finish. She hadn't seen so many bodies before, ever. She'd accepted the dangerous aspects connected with her job, but tonight's carnage was more than anything she'd ever experienced.

"I understand how you feel," Luke said, quietly. "You just have to take it a day at a time and let the memory fade."

She recalled the look in his eyes. "You speak as if you've lots of experience in this kind of thing," she said.

"I killed two people for you tonight," he reminded her. "I think the least you could do is share some information with me so we could figure out what's happening."

True. He was looking for Drei and Drei had been helping her when he disappeared. So, actually, they were both looking for a friend.

"Okay," she finally said. "Drei was helping me get certain items to free my father."

"Your father?" He sounded surprised. "I thought he was under protection in England?"

Nina shook her head. "Not any longer. An unknown group of terrorists have kidnapped and hidden him away somewhere. They communicated with MI6 that they're interested in negotiating an exchange deal and full usage of an MI6 contractor in Estonia for a year."

"But you weren't a contractor. You were in chicken farming."

"True. There was no way the English would give full access as well as pay for one year's service of a contract agent either, so they refused. My father gave them the name of a *La Niña*, a fixer with a reputation of getting difficult negotiations done quickly. *La Niña* was the code for my family when we were allowed to move to the States, so MI6 contacted me to work with them. I go undercover and make records of all the jobs I'm requested to do so we could figure out the items the terrorists were after. We all knew it was going to be a big job because they were willing to wait a whole year to implement whatever they're planning."

"But why would your father do that?"

"If I tell you, you have to reply to my question in good faith. What is Drei to you and why are you looking for him? And don't lie. You knew the location of Drei's house and where he kept his precious bike. Not many people do."

Drei was very private about that place. He had a business address for most of his contract jobs and another house he "lived" in, a huge converted medieval monstrosity he called his "party house." It was a noisy place, with many questionable characters walking in and out of it all the time. It had quite a reputation in Tallinn.

Luke drove silently for so long, she was beginning to wonder if he'd decided not to share information after all. She pushed back the unexpected niggle of disappointment. It was okay. She'd worked alone for so long, she would deal with this herself, although a part of her really, really wanted Cowboy by her side. Her attraction for him had been for so long and now that she had spent time with him, she wanted it to continue.

"He's my half-brother."

Of all the answers, she hadn't expected that one. "Half-brother," she repeated. They were both tall, dark and ridiculously handsome but looked nothing alike. Whereas Luke wore cowboy boots and sometimes a hat, she couldn't see Drei in either. She shook her head. "That's hard to believe."

"My mom is from Georgia, the one here in Europe. She had a son before meeting my dad, who, at that time, came over to sell farm equipment," Luke explained. "We aren't very far apart in age and grew up together on a farm in Georgia, USA. From Georgia to Georgia, see. Can't make that up."

"Yes, but wow. Drei, a farmer's son." The Drei she knew was a wild, carefree man, with very cosmopolitan tastes. "Okay, so I understand now why you suddenly showed up in our little black market corner of the world as the Cowboy. As a fixer, you could get information and you were trying to find him."

"Exactly. And every little bit of information I get or try to retrieve, I realize now, is linked to you. You're always around, even when you were not actually involved in what I was doing." He huffed out a sigh, as if letting the realization sink in. "My contact had been chasing clues about things Drei had connection with and of course, you're the connection. I was just too blinded by lust to figure that out."

Nina sat up. "Wait. Blinded by what?"

Luke glanced at her again. "Like you haven't known all along how much I wanted you. You and I have been eye-fucking for months, Nina. If you deny that, I'm going to have to stop the car and show you all the things you made me think of doing to you all this time."

That threat made her smile. She had teased him a lot. It was the only outlet of personal pleasure from her months of self-imposed control. She'd figured it was harmless fun, since the Cowboy appeared to be focused on his own thing. People in their business knew everyone's boundaries and from her agency, she'd learned that the Cowboy had a reputation of keeping to himself and making money on behalf of third parties who needed his expertise.

"Talking about stopping the car," she said, "are you going to ever stop somewhere? I need to pee."

She laughed at the look he gave her. She did enjoy teasing him so.

"I'm trying to make sure we aren't followed," he told her.

"I gather that, but I was wondering if you have a plan." She picked up the laptop by her. "You see, my handler's laptop had my personnel page front and center when he was killed while sitting at his desk. Why would he need my info up unless his killer made him? So I'm thinking those bastards were actually after me, but I only managed to access a few pages before they were blocked."

"I think they want you for the items you have been retrieving for your terrorists."

Nina frowned. "That's impossible. I don't have them. Everything is given to my company who works out the deal with their clients. I get the money wired in my bank account as soon as an item is exchanged or returned. You know how this works. Before Drei disappeared, we worked out, from all the jobs I've done this year, three items went to the men who are holding my father. Drei went off to the Ukraine to confirm one piece of our puzzle before he went dark. Last month, I've figured out the fourth object and—"

"What is it?"

She thought of the envelope secured inside the lining of her jacket. "I failed to deliver something tonight," she told him. Why were they in such a hurry that they chased her all over the city if that was indeed the last item? After all, they had waited almost a year for their project. Of course, the man she was supposed to pass the envelope to hadn't shown up. She tapped on the laptop. "Stop somewhere quick. I need to find a way to override a password or to see what those men really want from me, Luke."

"I know just the guy," Luke told her. "To get him, you have to be partners with me, sweetheart. It's connected to Drei and I want to find him."

Partners? Nina smiled up at the handsome face. "Is that all? Partners?"

"With benefits," he emphasized, returning the exact same smile she was giving him.

"Is this guy you know that good?"

"He found out all that stuff about you."

Nina tapped the laptop again. "These benefits better be good," she warned. "I'm very particular about benefits."

"Then I should show you how good they are," Luke drawled, his voice deep and sensual. "My digger is good but even he takes some time to crack computer software. While he's working, we can discuss your options."

She sniffed. "What is it with you and options, anyway?"

"An Airborne Ranger always outlines three choices, sweetheart. Option three is always the best one."

* * *

Luke called Konstantin before taking Nina up to their apartment. He knew his friend would still be up, either at his role-playing computer game or at work digging for information.

"No way are you bringing *La Niña* up to our place without going through the security wand," he said.

"Kostya, we need your help," Luke said.

"Oho, then she definitely needs to be wanded," his friend retorted. "I don't care how much into her you are. She's *La Niña*. She'd be insulted if I didn't show some concern for my safety."

"Hang on." Luke turned to Nina. "My friend wants to make sure you aren't bugged. He has a security wand and some kind of machinery that checks for high-tech weaponry. Usually, he isn't this restrictive with my friends, but you have a reputation, sweetheart."

"What, he wants to strip-search me?" Nina asked sarcastically.

"No, that's *my* job," Luke said.

She sighed. "You seem to only have that on your mind."

It was true. It was Nina naked all the time in his head, even during times of danger. She'd always been hot from afar but not tonight. Tonight, she had been his, just like in his dreams. He didn't care how much danger she brought with her. She was just dangerously hot and he was the man to handle her.

"Konstantin is extra careful because he isn't sure why I'm bringing you up, that's all. I haven't ever brought anyone back before, you see."

She raised a disbelieving brow at him. "Ever?"

Luke shook his head. Life here had been all about his search for his brother and his job had kept him too busy to entertain any social life. "I'm a lonely, lonesome, quite-alone soul," he said. He showed her his cell phone. "Should I suggest we don't stand around by the road all night where we could be seen? Coming up or not?"

"All right. As long as he understands I'll kill him if he touches me, even with a wand."

Luke resumed his conversation with Konstantin. "Kostya, she says yes."

"I think the lonely, lonesome, quite-alone line was what convinced her, my friend," Konstantin said from the other end. "I can't believe you're bringing *La Niña* home to me. Do you know how much money she could make me? There's a price on her head, you know. Someone placed an ad on an online dark site, saying it was urgent. I've been expecting you tonight, so I've got all my toys ready."

And that was just like Kostya to drop that bombshell out of nowhere. Luke could see the smirk on his face as he said that line. Hell, he was probably rubbing his hands in glee, anticipating some cyber digging fun.

Luke turned to Nina. "We have to go up now," he said, matter-of-factly. "You're wanted in the market."

The market was lingo for black market, of course. Nina's eyes widened. To be wanted in the market held many meanings, none of which was pleasant. However, his girl remained unruffled.

"Good to know," was all she said.

When they reached upstairs, Konstantin was already at the door, looking more unkempt than usual. He shook Nina's hand.

"Sorry about this," he said. "Luke told me there was a laptop. Please can you deposit it into my bag with your phone and any other e-devices you might have?"

After giving him a questioning glance, to which he responded with an encouraging nod, she handed over the laptop and took out several cell phones from her jacket.

"What about my gun?" she asked.

"You can keep that on you," Konstantin replied as he put the laptop into a clear plastic bag. "I'm going to scan it with my special box to the right of the door. Luke, you can wand her for me. You've seen me do it, right?"

"Yes. Can you order us some room service? I'm hungry."

Konstantin smiled. "I like her, Luke."

Nina stood by and watched as Konstantin placed her laptop and phones into a small box.

"What's that?" Luke asked.

"My homemade scanner," Konstantin replied. "Don't worry, it won't harm the devices. So the wand didn't find anything on the lady?"

"Nope, she's clean," Luke assured him.

Meanwhile, the scanner hummed a warning, with some buttons flashing red.

"But her laptop and phones aren't," Konstantin said.

"She picked the computer up from her office," Luke told him, "so I'm not surprised if it's loaded with bugs."

Konstantin stared at the e-pad in his hand, then turned to Nina. "My reader here tells me at least one of your devices is contaminated. Do I have your permission to disengage it?"

"What would it do?" Nina asked.

"Depends on whether it's the laptop or any of your cells. In the case of the laptop, it could just be a virus. If it's the phone, it might be loaded with a signal. I can jam that and keep you from being tracked."

"In that case, you have my full permission to do what you can," she said. She turned to Luke. "I'm hungry and need a snack. If you don't' feed me soon, I'm going to be very grumpy. You don't want to ever see me grumpy."

"I'll feed you," he said.

While they sat around a table eating soup and crackers, Luke filled Konstantin in about what had happened. He left out certain parts, of course, but his friend's eyes were filled with amusement because it was obvious to him what he and Nina had been up to.

Konstantin asked a few questions but other than that, he mostly kept busy playing with the pad controlling the scanner. Nina's computer and gadgets were still inside it being "cleaned," as Konstantin explained.

"It's going to take some time for me to look inside the computer and play with the software," Konstantin told them. "You both look like hell, so why don't you two get some sleep while I work?"

Luke checked the time. It had been a very long night. "I hope you can get in it quickly, Kostya. We don't have much time. We need to check the list of things Nina had delivered and see if there are addresses or individuals. We know the four things and Nina thinks she has the fifth in an envelope she's carrying."

"What's in it?" Konstantin asked.

"She hasn't shared that with me yet," Luke answered.

"I haven't had time to open it," Nina said. He watched as she unzipped a secret compartment in her jacket and pulled out a small, square envelope. "The man changed to a later time to meet and then didn't show up. I was heading back to HQ when you...um...delayed me."

He couldn't help giving her a wink. Then he realized something. "I saved you twice," he said. "If you'd gone back, those guys looking for you would have timed it just right."

Nina nodded soberly. "Yeah. I'd have met with the same fate as all my friends." She stirred her bowl restlessly. "The thing I don't understand is, they came back for me a second time, as if they knew I was in there. How did they know?"

That was exactly what was bothering him too. "They've been tracking you all along," he said. "They knew you were at Drei's and then they located you when you stopped at your office. I'm not sure how they did that exactly but the method has a delay involved, since each time, they hadn't shown up immediately."

"It was as if they weren't actually following me, you know?" Nina ran a hand through her hair. "You wanded me just now, so we know I haven't picked up some kind of bug they planted. It's not on my devices. So, how?"

He noted for the first time her eyes were red-rimmed. "You're tired," he said. "We're going to take that nap while Kostya gets to work. Are the cameras on in case we get tracked all the way here?"

Konstantin groaned. "That's all I need. My place riddled with bullets. Why did I have you as my roommate again?" He took another look at his scanner. "Honestly, I think it's one of those phones she's been carrying. The laptop wasn't on her until just recently, correct?"

"Right."

"Jackpot then," Konstantin said. He waved his hand dramatically. "Nina's phones can't give any signals while they're in my special magic box, my friends. You may go to bed and catch forty-winks whilst Sir Constantinos casts a circle of protection spell around us."

Nina gave Luke one of her looks. Oh yeah, he would need to explain to her about his friend's weird online character. But, right now, he was taking her to bed as soon as possible.

"Let's look at the contents in your envelope," he said.

Nina carefully tore it open. There was a tiny clear plastic case inside. She passed it around the table. Four ampoules filled with some kind of liquid were encased within the case.

"Let's not open it," he said. "I have a feeling these are not vitamins."

"I don't think so either," Nina agreed. She hid a yawn behind a hand. "Maybe they're energy pills."

"I'll see what's in the market that would fit the description of liquid-filled bullets," Konstantin said. "The case holding them is made very securely, so I'm thinking let's not try to open it like some stupid thieves would."

"Agreed. So, can we leave you to do your thing for a few hours?" Luke tugged Nina to her feet. "Let's get some rest."

"Bathroom?" she mouthed.

"Over there, down the hall. My room is the one to the right."

"Yes, I need my alone time now, folks. I'll bellow when I find anything," Konstantin said, picking up the box and heading for his study. When Nina disappeared into the bathroom, he added, in a low snarky voice, "Well, well, well. The Cowboy and *La Niña*, sitting on a branch."

"Sitting in a tree," Luke corrected.

"K-i-s-s-i-n-g," continued Konstantin, ignoring the correction. "Is love next?"

"I thought you said you needed your alone time, as you call it?"

Kostya did a little jig. "First comes love, then comes marriage, then comes baby in a baby carriage."

"You've gone cuckoo," Luke said, mildly irritated by the teasing. "I'm heading to the guest bath to wash up."

"Denial is a river in Egypt, my friend," Konstantin retorted with a wide grin. "You got her in your bedroom. Sure you're going to rest."

After freshening up, Luke knocked on his bedroom door and entered. Every good intention fled out the window at the sight of Nina lying on his bed in her bra and panties.

"What are your options now, Cowboy Ranger?" she mocked.

Option Three had never sounded so damn good.

* * *

Nina was tired of playing games and out-thinking opponents. Living on the edge, patiently making deliberate moves, sacrificing her needs because the end goal of saving her father was important. She'd followed MI6's instructions and played the role—stealing, retrieving, passing information and things of import—because they had needed to figure out the reason they were keeping her father prisoner and alive, but the British agency was just as secretive with her as with the terrorists. Drei, whom they'd hired to help for one retrieval, was the only one who had stepped up and helped her as much as he could.

She was tired. She wanted answers, especially now that everything had gone to hell. She'd almost died tonight and if not for Luke, she probably would have, or at least been seriously injured. Of course, going into this job, she'd been prepared to die, but damn it, she was this close to solving the mystery and saving her father. Why couldn't these stupid agencies be upfront about anything? Maybe MI6 was just as clueless at its end and was using her as a pawn, getting as much information from her unexpected talent while they could, before the inevitable.

Nina wanted to howl in frustration. Taking a deep breath, she took off her clothes and set them on a nearby chair. Deep breaths. Deep breaths. There was really nothing she could do but take control of her emotions and remain Nina, the remote and clever operative working for a MI6 fake, black market company in Estonia. It was clever, really, doing black market business as a front and finding out what the underground was up to. Everyone was a pawn and she was the idiot pawn, playing both sides on her own.

Well, she was tired of being alone. Tonight showed her how tired she was. And alone. Luke St. James, the man who had haunted her dreams this past year, had, within a span of hours, made her feel alive again. She'd laughed and oh yes, she'd actually enjoyed herself.

She stretched out on the bed, wondering about the man coming in. She had an idea what they would be doing other than sleep. One thing she was sure about—if she were going to die, she must first get to see Luke St. James naked and spend the little bit of time left with that delicious man. Nina the spy cautiously approved. Her real self, Naya, totally, enthusiastically approved. All settled, then.

The door opened. She struck a sultry pose.

"What are your options now, Cowboy Ranger?" she asked.

Her dream man did exactly what she'd hoped for. No words. Just that devilish smile with the hint of reckless abandon she'd always been drawn to. He started taking off his clothes.

He started with the black tee that snugly hugged that broad chest she'd wanted to explore. Oh. My. Nina pushed up against the pillow so she could comfortably watch. He was lightly tanned all over, like he spent time outdoors without his shirt, his color stayed with him through the colder months too.

There was nothing sexier than a muscular and fit man wearing nothing but jeans, especially one with molten heat in his eyes, devouring her with that male gaze. Every fiber in her body tingled at that look. She was glad he wanted her just as badly as she did him.

His jeans dropped to the floor and he stepped out of them. Nina stayed very still as he stalked towards the bed, his fierce arousal jutting out. Coming for her. She had never seen anything more beautiful.

"I got to see The Cowboy naked," she said lightly, her voice sounding unnaturally breathless. She needed to diffuse the tension she felt inside. "I can die happy now."

He climbed over her. "You aren't going to die, Nina," he informed her in a deep voice. "Unless you mean *la petit mort*. In that case, I can help with that."

"Mmm, promises, promises," Nina taunted. She didn't want to think about serious stuff right now. "Fuck me, Cowboy. Do it right this time. The first one earlier was too quick for my liking. In fact, let me show you how it's done."

She pushed against him and he obediently went onto his back. Sitting astride she admired the hard-on between her legs, waiting so patiently for her. It was gorgeous, if she could call a cock gorgeous—golden and smooth, with a beautiful head. She fisted the base of his penis and pulled the skin until it was taut and with her other hand, caressed his balls. He lay there, his lower body straining slightly, his breathing uneven. She smiled sensuously.

"I have a deadline looming and I need to come very badly, so the foreplay will have to wait, darling," she said.

"Foreplay can be a later option," he said, his voice gravelly with desire.

Putting her weight on her knees, she slowly guided him inside her, pushing down, all the while pulling gently at his balls. Luke muttered something but she didn't pay attention, too intent on the feeling of fullness as he slid inside. Letting go, she put her hands on his chest and started rocking up and down.

She could feel his thudding heart. Moving her hips rhythmically, she leaned over and licked his golden skin. Yum. His hand came up on her lower back, urging her down further. Another warm hand guided hers to her clitoris.

"Touch yourself," he ordered.

She slid her finger against her nub, slick with her own damp desire, rubbing in time with her long slide down. Every glide brought an extra trill of pleasure as she writhed against her finger. He started moving his hips in time with her and it felt like she was riding the best stud in the whole...then his fingers joined hers, pressing down on her clitoris.

The building orgasm that was balling white hot in her stomach burst into flame. It was a double pleasure, teasing herself outside and his cock caressing her inside. She moaned, bucking wildly. She was so wet, her essence marking him. *Mine*, she thought. *Mine, mine, mine.*

Nina fell forward, coming hard, calling his name. Suddenly she was on her back and he was on top, riding her now, thrusting in deep. Her orgasm continued in waves, her inner muscles clenching and unclenching, milking that hot cock inside her as it slid against her sensitive core.

With a groan, he gave her one hard thrust and came, pushing in so deep, she had to wrap her legs around him and hold on while their bodies shook uncontrollably.

This was what she had wanted to do with him for months and months.

It was worth the wait.

CHAPTER SEVEN

*T*hey slept, tangled in each other's arms. Luke woke up several times, thinking of what she'd told him and of his brother, trying to figure out how everything tied together. He watched Nina. She was soft and yielding in sleep, one hand tucked under her cheek like a child. He wanted to keep her by his side.

"Guys, wake up." Konstantin's voice called out through the door. "I need you out here ASAP."

Nina stirred.

"We're up," Luke said loudly. "Will be there soon."

"Hurry up! I've got answers!"

Luke caressed Nina's face gently with the back of his hand. Her eyelashes fluttered and she smiled.

"I don't want to wake up," she murmured.

"Me neither."

She opened her eyes sleepily. "Car chases tire me out," she said.

He chuckled quietly. She was even amusing in the morning. "And here I thought it was me."

She cuddled in for a kiss and he obliged. Her mouth was soft under his, but her response was bold and challenging. Her tongue teased his, inviting him to play and he did so. He ran his hand down her body slowly, first cupping one breast, then sliding down the soft womanly curves to rest between her legs. She responded to his touch there too, dampening his hand.

"Hey, we're supposed to wake up," she reminded him huskily before gasping softly.

"That's what I'm doing, waking us up," Luke said. He really liked watching her slowly going wild while he aroused her with his fingers. He circled her clitoris counter clockwise. "I can do this all day and keep you at my mercy."

"That sounds kinky," she whispered. "Can you go faster? Oh. Yes, like that."

There were a few seconds of silence as he brought her higher. He rubbed her a little faster and she moaned. When she came, he prolonged her orgasm, lightly scissoring that sensitive little pearl and massaging around it.

He decided watching a woman let go and come was the best way to start the day. He'd just satisfied his fantasy woman. Bring on reality then.

It was another half hour before they joined Konstantin in the kitchen. He pointed to the coffee pot.

"Leftover pizza for breakfast. Sorry." He patted the pile of papers on the table. Next to them was Nina's procured laptop. "Unlike you two, I've been working."

Luke rubbed his stubble. "About time you do that instead of playing your stupid treasure-hunting game," he said dryly.

"Ha. You guys are doing the same thing too. All these items?" He patted the pile next to him again. "They are like little bits of clues to some treasure. You're after some, she's after some, and there are others in this big game too. What we need to do is figure out what the treasure is."

Nina sipped her coffee. "Did you really manage to hack into the laptop? You did? What did you find out?"

Konstantin huffed out indignantly. "That's what I've been trying to tell you. I have clues to the treasure. We have a set of characters—you, Luke, the terrorists, even MI6, as well as an assortment of others. I've been mapping out who is who all night."

Luke shook his head at Nina's puzzled glance at him. "To understand Kostya, you have to speak his language," he explained sardonically. "Everything is about a quest to him right now."

"But it's true, she is on a quest! You both are," Konstantin exclaimed. "She's trying to free her father and you're looking for Drei. And these quests are intermingled with lots of black market magic."

Luke sighed and taking out the pizza he'd just heated up from the microwave, he placed one on a plate for Nina and handed it to her. He sat down beside her.

"Fine," he said. "Tell us about the black market magic."

Konstantin smiled. "First, let me show you how those evil wizards tracked you last night." He pulled out a cell phone, one Luke recognized was Nina's. "That's the magic wand." He tapped on some keys on the laptop. A page came up. "This is a password-protected key to your phone. Every time you reply to a text from your headquarters, it unlocks your exact location on this map. Your masters have been making sure you were where you said you were, Nina. All you had to do was acknowledged their text."

"Damn," Nina said, looking at the screen. "So they know when I was with Drei because I remember texting them. And last night, I did acknowledge their buzzing me while I was...busy."

Luke kept a straight face. She'd been busy all right. "When did you do this?" He asked, trying to keep the amusement out of his voice.

She looked back at him with an innocent expression. "When you were carrying me up the stairs. The phone was in my back pocket and I managed to click on it. I knew they would buzz me since I hadn't contacted them after my assignment. I wanted them to know I was okay."

"Was he really carrying you?"

Konstantin bellowed out a long bout of laughter. Luke knew he would find that amusing, since he had been acting so coolly whenever the subject of *La Niña* was brought up.

"Kostya, we need you to hurry this along," Luke said when the hoots died down a little. "We're under pressure here."

"Right. Okay, then, you ready? I think your pursuers were after Nina for her envelope. Unfortunately, you started carrying her up the stairs or something and thus stopped her from going back to her Headquarters where they'd assumed she would be. So, they had your handler find out where you were and by acknowledging his buzz, they had your location through the tracking software. I could show you, except I've disengaged the device. I'm not chancing them buzzing it with some other magical program."

"Good," Luke said. "Now what about the envelope?"

"I looked at all of Nina's runs through the last year and cross-referenced them with the times you also made similar runs. There are several reasons why you keep bumping into each other. One, you were both looking for Drei. Two, I was piecing together clues of this quest she is after and passing you what I've found out, except that we both couldn't see what was right under our noses."

"What?" Luke and Nina asked together.

Konstantin pointed at Nina. "Her. She was your quest all along, not your brother."

"Okay, you lost me, buddy," Luke said.

"It's like this. Drei disappeared while helping her but she and he have been sharing information about things she had been collecting. So everything she was after had a little Drei touch to it. I, the Great Constantinos, was looking for anything connected to Drei to help you out."

Luke nodded. "Yeah, I see it now. We were both looking for Drei, like you said, Nina was the one with most of the answers because she was working with him."

"He was just giving me a hand," Nina said. "But we managed to look at all my little errands and pick out the exact things those terrorist wanted."

"Oooh, I actually know the answer to that," Konstantin said, glee in his voice. "You see, all I have to do is look at the master file in the laptop indicating the clients. There were five items going to the same guy."

Nina swallowed her food. "Go on," she said.

"A political document of some sort. A photo. Someone even made a copy on your file, Nina. It's some kind of meeting at a café. Three men and a woman. The next was a small notebook with dates inside showing government meetings. Again, someone scanned all the pages into your file. The one before last night was Number Four, a glass with a fingerprint you stole."

Nina nodded. "Wow," she said, turning to Luke. "He's really good at this."

Luke finished the second piece of pizza. "Not that big a deal. All the time I paid him my hard-earned money, he only found tidbits with no real connections. Now he's got a laptop with a whole list to cross-reference, sure he's good."

"Hey, I was good too," Konstantin protested indignantly. "I gave you the biggest clue, *La Niña* herself. You were just too damn interested looking at her."

"That's true," Luke agreed. He'd been looking and looking. And looking. And now, he had her. He could afford to be generous. "Tell us about Number Five then."

"It's going to cost you," Konstantin warned. "It's big and I feel obligated to make some money for my extra hard work."

Luke gave a loud sigh. "Kost—"

"I could get MI6 to pay you," Nina interrupted. "One of those phones belongs to my contact there. He's very interested in making sense of all these quests too, I bet. With the way the damn agency has kept me in the dark, we'll make them pay. Let's ask for top Euros."

Konstantin nodded enthusiastically. "Wow," he gushed. "She's really good at this too. She'd make a great quest partner. We exchange clues and information in my online game a lot, Nina. Feel like joining me?"

"There's this matter of several people's lives being in danger here," Luke reminded his friend. Sometimes, Kostya lost his concentration and had to be pulled back in. "Number Five?"

Konstantin rolled his eyes. "It's the envelope."

"I know that," Luke said, "but what is it? Did you see what's been on the market?"

"Cross-referencing is the new black, my dear friend," Konstantin mocked, crossing his arms. "I looked at locations and then checked the usual requests on the black market sites. I believe I've discovered two things—where Nina's father is hidden and what those ampoules are."

Nina had dropped her plate when she heard what Konstantin said. Her excitement warmed Luke's heart. He could tell she was trying to hide how much Kostya's words affected her. Konstantin didn't miss it either.

"He's still in England," he said, the tone of his voice gentler now. "Maybe you can tell that to your contact and they can save him. They need to get the terrorists for sure. They're after someone big and they mean to kill him. Luke, those ampoules are poison and there's no way to safely get rid of them. The specific black market item wanted by the same group or individual is Polonium-210."

Luke stared at his roommate, then at the plastic package in the middle of the table. Polonium-210 was lethal radiation poison. A very small dose ingested would make a person die a slow and painful death by radiation poisoning.

"Someone in that photo connected to the dates in that black book will be assassinated," he said with quiet certainty. "We need to contact someone about this."

CHAPTER EIGHT

"Kostya, are you sure MI6 can't track you at all?" Nina asked. "Because he did not look very happy with our demands."

She had Luke to thank for Konstantin. The man was a gift. During the last two days, he'd helped send out secret messages to MI6 about her father's location. Saving her father was Number One, she'd told them. Then they could talk.

It took one day before she received a call on the special satellite phone they'd given her. It was her father's voice at the other end. He reassured her in code that he was alive and well, but unable to talk too much. No matter. He would get online and they would talk soon. She was just relieved he hadn't been harmed.

"Mother is fine," she told him. "Is there a reason why these men kidnapped you specifically?"

"Naya, your father knows many names of powerful men and defectors, and I'll leave you on that note."

Her father liked to refer to himself in third person when someone was listening in. It was a private warning to her and her family. He'd sacrificed his freedom so they could live freely. One day, she vowed, she would get him out, and he'd be able to walk anywhere without looking over his shoulder.

Somehow, using her phone, Konstantin also managed to get her and MI6 in a face-to-face conversation via computer. The half-hour negotiation was exactly what she needed to reestablish control. They had the Polonium-210 in their possession as well as all the information on the possible target.

"Your father is safe," reported the operative in a crisp British accent. "You can see it for yourself."

Her father, sitting quietly beside him, looked well enough. In front of him was his beloved chess set. He waved at her and moved a piece on the board.

Nina nodded. Her father was urging her to continue with this particular game. "Okay. Now, transfer the money so the digger who saved me gets paid. You know I'm going to need him to find out whose life is in danger."

"From your list, we think it's the Ukrainian president. Presently, we could only warn him of a possible attempt on his life, but he already knows this is likely since the Ukraine is in a state of war."

The Ukraine's civil war was taking its toll on international relations between Russia and many NATO countries. Everything was already hanging on a delicate balance. The NATO members didn't want another international incident that could create more political fallout. The fact that Russia was the main source of black-market Polonium-210 would certainly escalate the tension even further.

"Look, I'll do as you ask but only if you cover my partner too," Nina said. She shifted her gaze to Luke. He had gone very still at her announcement. "He has a missing friend he needs to find, so I need all the correct papers to cover his presence."

"A partner? When we sent you to Tallinn, we never sent you with a partner," the MI6 operative said, dryly. "Now we have to cover the cost of your friends too?"

"Do you expect me to enter the Ukraine by myself without a safety net?"

"Polonium-210 has a short half life," the British man pointed out. "They have a very narrow window to attack."

Nina felt Luke moving to stand next to her. "Whoever is behind this whole plot has waited a whole year to implement this kill," he said. "They aren't going to just stop if there is no Polonium. There are other poisons. Your problem is to extract the assassin without causing an international ruckus. On the other hand, I need to enter that country quickly. Nina has no combat experience and you're asking her to go out there into a war arena. That's, how should I put it politely, bloody stupid. I've been an Airborne Ranger and have experience with war. For the price of two, you get to avoid putting boots on the ground over there. Fair exchange or not?"

Nina enjoyed it when Luke took charge like that. She could see her father intently staring back at the screen, a small smile lifting the corners of his mouth. He seemed pleased. The operative was looking off-screen for a minute before answering. Obviously, some higher-up was sitting out of camera view.

The agent returned his regard on the camera. "Fair enough," he said. "You get everything you've requested. The military plane leaves tonight. You'll find what you need then. Good luck, Nina. The chief of operations wants to congratulate you for your year's work. Very well done indeed."

When the screen went blank, Konstantin jumped up in excitement. "Why didn't you tell me The Wizard King is your father?"

Nina frowned. "What?"

"Your father! He had his board set up exactly that way when he and I have our conversations during my game. He is the Wizard King to my Krazy Knight, giving me protection as I go hunting for treasure. I formed a pact with him because he's really very knowledgeable about history, which is good, since the game gets really deep. Also, he passes on great information through our chess moves."

Nina smiled. She could see Konstantin was totally obsessed with his game. She must remember to ask her father what the heck he was doing playing Dungeons and Dragons online. "Ah yes, my father likes to talk with his chess pieces. You must have broken his code and that's why he tells you things. He enjoys having one up on MI6."

"I need to meet the man! He has the key to that great treasure I am seeking," Konstantin said earnestly, sweeping his hand dramatically. He affected a British accent. "My quest will take me to a magical object sought by many. I shall win the ultimate prize, with the world at my heels in an amazing race."

"Oh, brother," Luke groaned aloud. "Let's pack, *partner*, before he goes all medieval on us."

He drawled out "partner" in a sexy twang, making Nina giggle. She found it hilarious when he did his country boy act—cowboy hat tilted to hide his face, hands on belt, one booted leg crossed over the other. Last night she made him do just that while standing naked. Good Lord. A naked cowboy who looked like that should be against all laws of decency. She had slowly and deliberately sauntered over to him then. He had continued to wait while she circled him. What followed probably did break decency laws. Many of them.

She grinned. "You like that," she noted.

"Yup. Partner sounds good," he agreed. He stepped closer. "I like it a lot. Thank you for getting me a fast ride to the Ukraine to look for my brother."

"Drei is a good friend," Nina said. "I want him back too. And stop looking at me like that. I meant I want him back as a friend. We never did anything. He's too damn kinky, anyhow."

Luke cocked an eyebrow. "Kinky? My brother?"

"Your brother," she said, poking a finger at his chest, "likes women, as in two or three at the same time. Women seem to like to share him with each other. Me, I don't go for sharing, so you better remember that."

Luke laughed. "Drei does like to entertain himself like that. I remember one time we and the Lawrence quintuplets—." He cut off as if he realized what he was going to say would get him in trouble. He coughed, then continued, "Hmm...well. Farmer Lawrence's daughters gave some great parties."

"Uh-huh," Nina said. "Quintuplets."

"Quintuplets?" Konstantin chimed in. "Can I get an invitation to that party?"

Luke gave his friend a long look as he pulled Nina closer. "I really don't want you coming along with us.

Shouldn't you just stay here and continue your online role-playing quest?"

"You forget, I've amused myself for almost a year watching the two of you trying to outshine each other looking for your damn things. Nope. I can't miss all the fun." His expression sobered. "I can help find your brother, Luke. You'll need lots of electronic access and I can provide that."

"Hmm. How are you with jumping out of airplanes?"

"I can do that, no problem!" Konstantin whooped.

"Uh, what?" Nina asked, a puzzled frown creasing her forehead.

"Military plane, sweetheart. It sure ain't landing there. I have a feeling we'll be making a jump."

"No. Way." Nina crossed her arms. "I don't jump out of airplanes and definitely not in the dark! I mean, how would I know where I would land?"

"I'll bring a compass!" Konstantin said.

"We'll have to go tandem," Luke decided. "Me on your back, humping you. Hot."

"I'll bring a camera!" Konstantin added.

"It isn't going to happen!" Nina exclaimed, looking from one to the other. She backed away from Luke as he came for her, then squealed as he tossed her over his shoulder, just as he did that night when he kidnapped her. "Cowboy!"

"We're going to practice tandem maneuvers tonight, partner."

Nina could only cling to that hot body with which she was growing too familiar. Partners with work and...tandem moving.

As they left the room, she heard Konstantin whistling the Kissing song. She and Cowboy sitting in a tree. Jumping off a plane. Maybe. Together, though. Yes, yes, yes.

"Can you really hump me from the back?" she wondered out loud.

Luke's sexy laugh sounded promising. Hot days and hotter nights ahead.

FINIS

Dear reader,

Thank you for reading my books. Naya and Luke begin a new partnership in Dangerously Hot. To subscribe to my newsletter, please send an email to Jenn@Gennita-Low.com with NEWSLETTER in the subject.

NOTES

1) Tallinn has always been a great city for espionage. The combination of modern high-tech systems and medieval building is fascinating. I love the wild, wild West feel to parts of Eastern Europe. Here is an interesting link about its history and its spy connection:
    http://www.bbc.com/travel/story/20111208-tallinns-secret-history-of-espionage

2) Polonium-210 is real. It has been suspected as the substance used to kill a Russian defector living in Britain, named Alexander Litvinenko, as well as Yasser Arafat. The idea behind this story comes from the combination of the above murders and the recent poisoning of another Eastern European leader. I hope to explore this further in the next "HOT SPIES" novella.

3) Double agents, special operatives and contract agents make up a lot of the busy underground network in Estonia. A Russian double agent was recently revealed in the Estonian spy agency after he was "kidnapped" back into Russia in 2014. The discovery caused a scandal since it was discovered

the operative had passed on NATO allies' secrets to Russian Intelligence.

4) You will find Drei making an appearance in a "HOT SPIES" novel titled SIZZLE. He's a contract agent and lives life on the edge so he'll be a fun one to write about!

SIZZLE
(Hot Spies 2)

by

Gennita Low

SIZZLE
BOOK 2
Hot Spies Series

by

GENNITA LOW

* * * * *

PUBLISHED BY:
GLow World

Sizzle (Hot Spies Series)
Copyright © 2015 by Gennita Low

Sign up for newsletters: Jenn@Gennita-Low.com

PROLOGUE

We didn't meet often, but every time I saw her, my brain went to my dick. Every. Fucking. Time. The way her big eyes looked at me. That half-pout of a smile. The slinky walk with those long, long legs.

I wanted her so badly.

At first, I chalked it up to her beauty. Some spies could turn people on with a look. Sex trappers, we called them. It was fine to play along and I'd been trained to do my job, get my own information and leave the other side alone. She had her own job and I had mine.

Our paths crossed so many times. We started to talk and became friends. If people like us could be friends. One thing led to another and we started flirting.

She made me laugh, which surprised me. She was light to my darkness, like a sliver of sunshine amid stormy clouds. I began to dream of seeing her more often. Sometimes, during the dark hours of watching and waiting—spies did that a lot—I'd idly fantasize about going dark, working on my own, and kidnapping and spiriting her away somewhere. She'd be all mine and I'd finally make love to her and spend time doing all the things I wanted to do with her.

It wouldn't be easy, what with today's technological advances, but it was possible. So, in the dark, during an operation, waiting for action, my mind searched for ways to be erased.

Tsun Tzu, in the Art of War, taught of there being five classes of spies: the local, the inward, the converted, the doomed and finally, the surviving spies. I used to wonder which class I belonged to, and which one I should work towards as a goal. I mean, even spies, cynical lot as we were, should have a few goals.

As a young man, I was interested in history and philosophy. I wanted to see the world and find out its secrets. Back then, it was more like: so this important person died in this country, so let's travel there and retrace the steps and see if I would agree with what the historians told me about this figure.

Now, at thirty-one, I realized I'd captured my dream in a perverted sort of way. My duties carried me around the world and gave me privilege to many of its secrets. There were important people running through my life all these years—people who had shaped history and given me a calling. We named it the game of cloak and daggers, but life and death wasn't a game for those of us in the field. It was a reality.

I'd lost friends. I'd given up loves. I'd ignored family.

Not any more. I could not lose her.

I'd come to a decision to create another class of spies. Not just a surviving spy, one who returned to give news to his master—I was already that many times over—but one who could erase himself. The disappearing spy. Yeah, some hokey term like that would do.

So, it started with my wanting to fuck this woman, this spy known to seduce with a look. Fucking was easy and I'd avoided that. Avoided it all so I could talk to her, to see what was behind that smoky voice and too-innocent face. In the end, I fell like a ton of bricks for her and the plan to be the disappearing spy had taken root.

Why would I do this, you ask? Cynicism, perhaps? Overgrown disillusion about the state of affairs in the world? Well, yes, partly that. But, the top reason would make Tsun Tzu very angry and disappointed with me as a soldier of the game. I did it...for love.

CHAPTER ONE

Lola cut her steak carefully into little bites. She popped a piece of meat into her mouth and enjoyed the burst of flavor on her tongue. She was sent here on "holiday," amid the chaos that was the Ukraine. Her other mission was to meet with a man called Stanov but that was later. Right now, she'd enjoy her "holiday." Right now, she'd sit quietly and contemplate whether her recent decision was too crazy.

She took a sip of her wine and looked out of the window to enjoy the view of the Azov seaboard. It was a nice hotel, undamaged by the unrest in the city. Outside, the ceasefire was holding. Here, she was given a room as a "guest" and there was enough staff left to take care of her needs.

What she needed wasn't here, though. But he would be soon.

Wouldn't he?

A part of her mind nervously played on her naturally suspicious nature. What if he changed his mind and didn't show up?

Then you continue with your job, came the quiet assurance. *It's not the end of the world*. Easily said but not easily believed. She'd known Jacob Travis long enough to know, if he didn't show up, it could only mean two things— he'd been found out and was prevented somehow to continue, or, he'd decided the risk wasn't worth it, and if the latter were true, then all his words had been lies, falsehoods to persuade someone from the opposite side to betray her job.

There were tensions between their countries, after all. It was the growing tension this past year that had decided their course of action. If they waited any longer, it'd be dangerous for them to talk as "acquaintances." Previously, an alliance was allowed here and there during operations of mutual benefit but the opportunities were getting fewer as both their sides were playing their version of Cold War spy games.

It was time, he'd said, when they'd last met. And her heart had bloomed like a flower at the thought of being with him, away from all this.

"Yes," she'd replied.

His smile back was so damn sexy. "Cannot wait."

That was a few months ago and with many dangerous messages hidden through various means, communicating the next location, the next possibility, they'd finally found the right place and the right time. And here she was, Lola Kalina, waiting to disappear with the man she loved.

A man entered the restaurant. Lola looked sideways. It wasn't him.

Although there was unrest in the area, there was a cease fire in place and people were venturing about the city, cautiously hopeful as they enjoyed a rare day without the sounds of shelling and gunshots. She felt sorry for Mariupol's citizens. Russians love to come here for their vacations and in happier times, she'd visited with a few friends. Now, there were Russians here with a different agenda.

She sighed. How did Jake put it? Sometimes, following orders sucked canal water. He'd made her laugh with that. Such a strange term. Exchanging silly colloquial terms, they giggled like kids sharing a secret.

There hadn't been much laughter in her life. It was a strict upbringing, with many rules and not much freedom. Even now, the freedom she had was a restricted kind. The first time she'd laughed spontaneously was when Jake put on the most ridiculous disguise at an assignment in which she'd been tasked to get someone's attention through the usual seduction. Jacob Travis had arrived dressed as a clown, big nose, big feet, the whole make-up, even an act. Nobody had recognized him but she did. The fake bald patch with the rainbow tufts of hair couldn't disguise the way he walked. He'd shown up, apparently at the wrong party, and started giving a show, even though there were no kids around. By the time the people came along to get him out of there, he'd already accomplished his task—handed off a balloon animal to a woman. No doubt, with a secret message in it.

Lola had enjoyed the ridiculousness of it all, so much so, she hadn't reported it to her superiors. The clown act was in direct contrast with her usual method, and had given her a few minutes of pure surprise, then laughter. She'd wished...she'd wished she could be a clown.

How odd was that moment? And yes, it was then she'd started feeling more than attraction for "that American spy," as she'd called him. His eyes had caught hers and his gaze had lingered for an extra moment. He'd then winked conspiratorially, as if daring her to expose him. He'd even leered at her, with his tongue hanging out. Wicked man.

She took another bite of her steak and then a sip of her wine. She frowned. Then smiled secretly, a glowing joy welling up her heart. It wasn't what she'd ordered but she'd tasted that particular drink before. He was here.

* * *

"This plan will get her killed."

Jake turned to look at the other man looking through the small two-way mirror in the office. Lola was sitting eight feet away, facing them, looking relaxed and enjoying her meal. She took a sip of her drink. Her brow furrowed a little, then a small smile appeared, as if she suddenly remembered something.

"I hope so," Jake said, quietly.

He couldn't take his gaze away, drawn to the way she was eating. Little bites. She picked a small cherry tomato and slowly popped it between her luscious lips, her tongue licking away the juice. He must remember to get finger food so he could feed her himself. He wanted to lick the juice off himself. In fact, he wanted to lick her all over. What would she taste like?

"If this plan fails, we will die," his companion interrupted his reverie.

Jake slanted Marco a glance, studying the demeanor of the other man. He didn't appear nervous or hesitant. Good. He didn't want someone who would change course from the original plan.

"Your side needs the information. I can't get this directly without attention."

"Too many news people," Marco agreed. "Can't have an American getting any mention in the news right now."

"We'll give them a story," Jake said. He nodded toward to Lola. "Her info will be good. Whether we succeed or not, the exposure alone would be worth it for your side."

Marco nodded. "True, but it'd be 100 times better if we could get our hands on the weapons."

"It'd be nice, but the Russians are wily. They layer all their information so I doubt Lola is the only one giving the whole message."

"If there are other women like her hanging around restaurants in Mariupol right now, all the 'Russian militia on vacation' are lucky men," Marco joked cynically. His fingers bracketed his phrase in quotation marks. It was well-known the Russians were using that term as an excuse to bring fighters into the city. "Where are all these pretty women, I wonder?"

Jake shrugged. He was only interested in one. "There will be different couriers. She is just one I know."

"What if she's a decoy? Then what?"

Jake had wondered about that. Perhaps he was just a foolish man to place his heart above his head, to really believe everything Lola had told him. It was too late now. He was going through with it, no matter what.

"Then I'll deal with her," he said. "Just one step at a time. We first trick Viktor. The rest follows."

Marco inhaled deeply, paused, then let out his breath slowly. "All right. We'll do it, but there are no guarantees she'll make it."

Jake nodded back. "You just leave her to me," he said.

He watched Lola finished her drink. She unwrapped a small piece of complimentary chocolate and bit into it. He'd made sure it was her favorite kind. Her face lifted and her smile of pleasure radiated all the way into his heart. Soon. Soon he would be part of that pleasure too.

"And so it begins," he murmured.

* * *

She had a text from her handler on her disposable phone. Her instructions for Day 1 were relatively simple. It was sent right on schedule, right after lunch.

You're on holiday. They're watching. Go shopping. Seduce someone tonight. Convince them you're there for fun.

The Ukrainians were looking for Russian infiltrators, soldiers coming in and then secretly joining the rebels. That was why they'd sent her. One might overlook a woman doing some shopping and having casual sex. She sighed. She knew she was being watched by both sides. If she didn't bring a man into her room that night, there would be questions.

The summer weather was perfect for market day. Despite the fear that the ceasefire wouldn't hold, the citizens were out, taking a chance to enjoy life and resume normalcy. Lola strode, casually stopping at a stall and moving on to the next, picking up scarves and sunglasses and donning them.

"You look like a movie star," the male voice said softly.

She looked across the sales table. A bearded man looked back at her, eyes behind sunglasses too.

"You should buy both," he said, with a smile, his teeth yellow from cigarettes. "Cheap, ma'am. I need the money."

She cocked her head. "Movie star?" She wrapped the scarf over her shoulder and struck a pose. "A famous one or one just starting out?"

"Ahhh. Well, a famous beauty, of course. Here, you should put it on like this," he said, leaning over and lifting the scarf off her shoulders and gently securing it around her face and flipping one side over a shoulder. "There, with the sunglasses, you're incognito from your fans."

His fingers brushed her neck as he tied a loose knot. The back of his hand smoothed down the rumpled material.

"I suppose I have to buy them now that you've put it on me so prettily," Lola said, taking a look in the mirror hanging over the table. "Here, keep the change."

"Thank you kindly, ma'am. Hope to see you again while you're here," the man said, taking the money from her.

Their hands touched fleetingly and his fingers lingered for half a second longer. She couldn't see his eyes but the smile was his, in spite of those ugly teeth.

"Maybe," she replied, smiling back.

"I wish I was handsome and young, so you won't be alone tonight," he flirted, bowing his head.

Her smile disappeared. She didn't want to think about tonight. She would prefer to fantasize about spending time seducing Jake, instead of picking up a stranger just to please her boss. It was something she didn't do often, but it'd been drummed into her ever since she was picked off the streets that her body was her weapon. Her trainers had taught her to go after targets using the art of seduction.

Jake had known about this. He'd once challenged her while they were at a "party" that he would get her wet just by talking to her. She had been making a circle around the room, making small talk to different people, passing on messages to two weapons dealers. He'd casually joined her in a conversation and in one of those times when they were alone, they'd flirted and he'd palmed her a card with a number when he kissed her hand.

Lola had called as soon as she knew no one was listening. He'd picked up on the second ring.

"It's me," was all she'd said and nothing else, as he started talking. After that she'd hung up without a word.

She'd needed a drink and a shower after he finished telling her what he'd do to her. Even now she could recall his softly spoken words—a masculine drawl, with a slight edge—told with that lilt that came with a born storyteller, the slow cadence of mesmerizing promises that were both arousing and terrifying at the same time.

I want to stand you in front of a mirror so I can see your face. I'd undress you—slowly—because every part of you is a treasure to me. I'll watch you in the mirror too, every part of you revealed to me, finally. Your breasts in my hands, the feel of their weight, the sensation of your nipples hardening as I rub them.

I'll move my hand down that flat stomach and put it between your legs. You'll lean back against me and feel my cock hard against your back, wanting you, needing you, like I've been doing every fucking time I see you. My hand will learn where to touch to give you pleasure. Wet pleasure. The kind only I can give you because I'll take the time before I fuck you, Lola. I'll take the time, watch your face in the mirror, know how many fingers you like, how much pressure to get you to part your legs wider, know how many strokes before you tremble and fall back, so all your weight is on me. I'll crush you to me as I watch you come, and as you melt, I'll lean you down against that mirror, so you can watch my cock pushing inside you, my hand still between your legs, still giving you that wet pleasure, and I'll fuck you hard because I can't do it slow the first time. Hard and fast and furious, with you watching my cock moving and fingers stroking, feeling me deep inside as you melt around me.

And that's the beginning. The next thing's my mouth. You know what I want to do. On your mouth. On your breasts. On your hot, waiting pussy. Tell me I made you play with yourself after you hear this, and I'll tell you what I plan to do to you with my mouth.

Arousing because no man had ever spoken like that to her before. Seduction had never been from the other side and it'd always been all the act and none of the words. Terrifying because, behind his words, Jake had told her he wanted total control of her body, that he wanted her to let him seduce her. That last part was a leap of faith she'd never learned to take with anyone, and, most of all, with a man.

She'd just have to get through tonight, even though the thought of being with another man, when all she could think of was Jake, made her want to punch something. It was getting harder to compartmentalize her feelings. She'd been very careful these past months not to get distracted because of Jake and she had to plan very, very slowly. She didn't want her handler to notice anything out of the ordinary.

The one thing that had kept her focused and determined was Jake's private number. She had continued to call him on a throwaway cell phone just to hear him make those sexy promises. Words. She was being seduced by mere words. They haunted her, teased her, provoked her. Distracted her when she was supposed to be doing her job. When she was supposed to flirt with an assignment, she found herself thinking about Jake instead and wanting to be with him.

Tonight would be the last time, she swore. She wanted to be with Jake and no one else. It was dangerous to put all her trust in his hands, but she would make that leap of faith, fall into his arms and let him take her wherever he wanted. She wanted to be Jake's woman and only his.

CHAPTER TWO

The current ceasefire between the rebels and the Ukrainian army had given its citizens some hope that there would be peace. Restaurants and clubs reopened. The younger crowd was out in their vehicles, beeping, playing loud music and waving at everyone. There was an air of giddy festivity at the square.

Lola mingled with the crowd. Everyone wanted to party and have a good time. Even the few soldiers present looked relaxed, although she had the feeling they weren't there just to celebrate. There was still suspicion with anyone in town who might be Russians in disguise. The evidence had been real enough—many rebels had been heard speaking with a heavy accent and there were news reports of "vacationing" Russian military personnel showing up at hospitals with serious injuries. How they came to choose to holiday in a country split by civil war was a mystery to no one.

She'd kept it a secret when they'd taken her from her parents, but there was Ukrainian blood in her from her grandmother's side. So maybe it was fate she was here today, with a very important partial message to pass along.

No time to mull over choices. She took a deep breath, taking a few seconds to push away the personal part of her. It was an exercise in disengagement, like watching a stranger who looked like her go through the motions.

She exhaled slowly.

Then she casually swung her small purse over her shoulder and sauntered past the men in uniform and down the road toward a popular night club. She could feel their gaze following her as she stopped in front of the place and bopped to the music beat emanating from the entrance. A man outside the bar beckoned to her, encouraging her to go inside. She smiled and nodded, following him in.

"Why are you alone?" he asked. "Where are your girlfriends? We need girls!"

"I'm alone, sorry. Was invited here and got caught in this—you know—" She shrugged dismissively. "It was such a pretty day today, I can't resist going out. I should leave now that all the fighting has stopped but why not have a little fun before, right?"

"Right! And you can have fun here with my friends and me," the young man invited. "We're all off for the night too."

"Off?"

"Yes, from our duty in Donetsk."

"Oh, are you soldiers too?"

"Volunteers. Come on, let's go in and dance."

It was dark in the club, with the dance floor in the middle being its brightest place. The techno beat of the music was loud and it was crowded with people gyrating energetically. Colorful strobe lights punctuated the pounding beats and every now and then she could see smiling faces and waving arms.

"Crowded!" The man with her shouted over the music. "Everyone's happy the fighting's stopped."

She nodded and scanned the shadowy darkness. It was difficult to see anyone in here, although she had no doubt she was being observed. Certain quarters were checking out the visitors here in town. Besides her own people, the man she was supposed to meet with would have his men watching her too. Then there were the other spies, doing what spies do, knowing that a ceasefire was just a pause to gather information.

She let the stranger pull her towards the dance floor. His friends—a group of about six or seven—waved at him and he gestured for them to join him.

"Come on, come on! Let's party!" He called out as the dance floor swallowed all of them into its mix of moving bodies.

Lola didn't really feel like dancing, but her body moved on its own, letting the beat take over. Detached, as if she were suspended somewhere, she watched herself sway and twist, laughing as the man pulled her against his body.

Not yet. Flirtation and temptation first.

She untangled herself in a smooth move and did a little solo gyrating. The others crowded around her, clapping. She lifted her arms above her head, slow and sexy, then swayed forward a little, then took a few steps back. Her quarry followed, wanting more. She smiled, turned her back to him and did the same thing to the male there. He hooted. She twisted and turned again in a different direction. On time with the music, she sashayed in front of yet another man.

Establish control. Beckon an invisible finger.

She bent forward, ran her fingers slowly through her hair, and arched her back. She watched, with half-closed eyes as her men danced around her, each wanting to get lucky tonight. She edged slowly to one side of the floor. That was enough to show her observers she was just a girl having fun.

The strobe lights slowed down and dimmed to even more shadows as the beat slowed down to a sexy song. A hand snaked around her middle and pulled her back. Then she was against a solid body. She turned to look and found herself crowded into a corner, that same body crushing her against a shelf.

A hand tugged at her hair, jerking her head back. A hard mouth kissed her then nibbled along her jaw line to her ear.

"You think I'm going to let any of these bastards near you now? No one's going to have you but me," a familiar voice said.

Lola peered up at the face in the shadows. He had done something to his hair and a trim beard covered his usually clean-shaven jaw. He tugged her hair again, burying his face in her neck.

"They're watching," she told him. "I'm under orders to get a boyfriend for tonight."

"Let them watch. The way you were dancing, you were getting several boyfriends. They want you to be seen looking for men, they got their wish."

His voice was heated. His teeth bit her earlobe,

Knowing it was him changed everything. Her whole body, usually so in control, had gone limp and simply melted into his arms. This wouldn't do.

"We must be careful," she insisted. "They know my style."

"Yes, but they also want the local spies to think you're here for some male attention. Just going off that fast wouldn't make them less suspicious, my love. You must make an impression."

"An impression?" She wasn't sure what he meant. "Like how?"

"Like this."

He ground the lower half of his body against hers. His mouth closed over her gasp of surprise. Her skirt was swished up and she felt bare hands on her thighs. Without any warning, she was lifted off the floor and with her back against the wall, she couldn't do anything else but hug her legs around him for support.

Everything became a jumble of sensation. His scent. His taste. His arousal. His rigid length nudged hard against her through their clothes. She shook her head to free her mouth.

"Yes, fight me a little, so I can carry you out of here, baby," he growled, his stubble rough against her cheek. "Let my guys make a big deal about it so your side doesn't interfere."

His hand slid down the crack of her panties. She arched her back in shocked reaction. All these months, he'd never touched her, ever. A couple of quick stolen kisses were all they'd shared. He'd teased her with words, and it'd all been her imagination.

And now—

His hand was under her skirt, boldly exploring her in public. It was dark in this corner, but their provocative dirty dancing left little to the imagination. Her whole being pulsed with shock and desire. Questions raced through her mind, the foremost being this new Jake. He was acting cruder than she'd ever seen him. She tasted a little anger in his heated kiss and his caresses were—she closed her eyes—deliberately and steadily invasive. The man was trying...to...make...her come. In public.

"Why?" she asked. She dared not say his name out loud. "Why are you...?"

"Mine," he told her firmly. "Not theirs to order around. Not anyone to tempt. Just mine."

She gasped again. His firm touch was relentless. She could feel herself getting wetter, losing control. A finger slowly entered her, ruthlessly using her own growing desire against her, gliding sensuously over her sensitive nub. In the darkness, amid the music and male hooting behind him, Jake was staking his claim.

She'd never lost control. It would never do to let her handler find out about how she lost it on the dance floor. For some reason, Jake was being reckless, so she must be the cool-headed one here. Quickly, she laced her fingers behind Jake's neck and pulled him lower, kissing him deeper. Because he had to lean in, she knew he'd have to put one hand against the wall to brace his weight. Taking her opportunity at the sudden release, she lowered her feet from around his waist.

He lifted his head and gazed down at her. His face was stamped with something dark. Need and desire glittered in his eyes and she saw how close he was to losing control too. They wanted to be together so much that everything else appeared unimportant. It was crazy, this need that they'd kept at a sizzle for so long. One kiss in public and the heat had tripled.

"Dangerous," she breathed.

"I know," he said, then grasped her hand and turned to face his friends. "Let's get out of here. Lady and I want to party."

"Hey, she's with me!" the man at the entrance protested.

"Ach, Andre, come along," Jake said. "We'll both party with the beauty. Let's go to the apartment."

The others laughed and cheered and some, hugging some other women, followed them as they headed out, singing and yelling crudely at each other. Lola laughed and tugged at her man's jacket, wagging her forefinger at him. He put an arm over her shoulders. The other man, walking with them on her other side, demanded her attention too. In the midst of all this, she noted with interest there were partiers in front and at the back of her and, with her two "beaus," she was covered at all sides.

They all gathered outside and after a bit, two vans showed up, blaring loud music and honking. Lola laughed again as Jake carried her into the vehicle and a few others piled in after them. The door closed and the van started moving.

The other man—Andre, she remembered Jake called him—immediately took out a wand and, with a finger over his lips, started to wave it over her body. Lola understood. It was to make sure there weren't any listening devices on her. After a minute or two, he gave her and Jake a thumbs-up.

She turned to Jake. "What was that all about? It isn't what we planned."

Jake gave her a long look, then spoke in English. "I was helping you with your new orders." He cocked his eyebrows. "Make it look like you're here for a boyfriend."

"Yes, but—"

"Do you want to have someone else tonight?" The question was mildly stated but his eyes still had that glint.

Lola frowned. "Of course not, but it's still risky, you being seen in public."

"I told him that but he wouldn't listen," the other man said, in accented English, "so this is the new plan."

"Why won't you listen, Jake?" Lola asked softly. It was a really big risk. If someone had recognized him under that beard and cap....

"I don't want another man touching the girl I'm about to marry," Jake told her.

Lola stared at him. Then she blinked. "Was that a proposal?"

* * *

Fuck being professional. This was personal.

Possessiveness and jealousy, two very alien emotions in a spy's make-up. When Jake realized something about Lola was bothering him, it was too late to nip the growing feelings in the bud. Just like anything else, he'd thought he'd be able to compartmentalize, get these distracting feelings out of the way.

He'd been wrong.

Bottling his possessiveness and jealousy up had resulted in anger. Before, he'd been able to dismiss most of the resentment by telling himself this was work, that duty was important.

Fuck importance. This wasn't work or assignment or whatever the fuck he'd been telling himself. This was watching the woman, for whom he was about to give up everything, make a move toward another man. He didn't care how childish it was to want to stop that from happening. He would not let one of these "dutiful" acts be another step in their grand escape plan.

Lola might be able to go through with it, but he couldn't. Not this time. His friend tried to discourage him, but no, he changed the original plan because this was not a fucking job for him, and he didn't care if no one was going to help him prevent *his* woman from continuing with her instructions tonight. Fuck instructions. This was about their freedom, after all.

Jake looked at Lola. He felt as if he was filled to the brim with all the possessiveness and jealousy of a man in love. Words that he wanted, and hadn't been able to share, stuck in his throat, frustrating him even more. Beautiful, poetic words he'd wanted to share about being with someone for whom he cared.

None came out of his mouth. His planned speech was distilled into one frustrated sentence.

"I don't want another man touching the girl I'm about to marry," he blurted out.

Well, hell, fuck and hell again, Jake, my man. You're one fucking fine smooth talker there.

"Was that a proposal?" Lola asked.

Jake heard Andre's snicker. This wasn't what he'd planned but it'd have to do.

"I wanted to ask nicely later," he said.

Her smile always made his gut clench up. It lit up those dark eyes that peered up from under thick eyelashes. Did she know what power she had in that smile?

"Ask again later, then," she told him, then sat back with a sigh. "Now tell me who these people are and what we'll be doing the next few hours besides pretending to be having a *ménage à trois* with Andre?"

Andre snickered again. "We don't have to pretend, if you like," he came back, then lifted both hands up in surrender at Jake's growl. "Of course, I prefer two women naked with me instead of his asshole in my way."

Lola laughed. "I like him," she told him, with a wink. Then, studying him for a moment, she leaned forward, lightly scratched his fake beard, and whispered, "I like you much, much more, even with a beard and ugly hat. Stop being a grouch."

And just like that, the tight fist around his heart loosened a little. Only she could do that to him.

"Here, *amigos*, maybe a shot of Vodka will calm you down some," Andre offered, tossing a bottle in his direction.

Jake caught it and popped the top open with his thumb. He took a generous swig, feeling the fiery liquid slide down his throat into his belly.

"All right now?" Andre asked.

"Everything's under control," Jake lied. He was fine, as long as he didn't let himself think about Lola almost being with another man.

"Let's fill the lady in, then. My name is Andre, as you know. I'd be what Americans call an independent contractor."

"You speak English with an American accent," Lola noted.

"That's because I'm American. Second generation, or 1.5, if you want to be technical about it."

"What do you mean?" Lola asked.

"Don't let him get started about his background and familial roots or we'll be getting a history lesson," Jake warned. "Let's just leave it at independent contractor, working for my side."

"Okay," Lola said. "Is he the one whose identity I'm going to release?"

Jake nodded. "If the timing is right, the Russian military will go in search of the location I gave you."

It was a stop-gap measure, a gamble to delay another attack while the international principals negotiated a form of peace treaty. As long as the ceasefire held, there was hope.

They couldn't stop the delivery of weapons without violence, so the international agencies had decided the best course of action was to delay the fake Russian "aid" convoy somehow. However, they must first remove the military element, which tended to be more aggressive in their reactions. If they were out of the area and unable to get back in time, Mariupol and thus, Ukraine, might be spared another battle.

Everything rested on Lola. They knew she was going to meet with a Russian militia agent. She would be telling the truth, so she wouldn't be betraying her country. The subterfuge lay in the delay and this piece of information was kept from her. The less she knew, the safer she would be.

"Show me the maps again. I'll memorize it," Lola said. She looked around. "I really hope there's a party we're going to because you realize we're being followed, right?"

Andre smiled. "There's a party. You two will have some privacy to...discuss...your plans." His smile dimmed. "Pray too, that everything will work out."

They were both balancing on a very tightrope of their own, trusting each other not to betray their sides. No one, except Andre—damn his wily mind for guessing the truth—knew their biggest secret here, that at the end of this operation, they'd be gone.

He glanced at Lola and discovered she was studying him too, gauging his reaction. He leaned in to give her a quick, reassuring kiss. Her head tilted back, welcoming him.

"You're the answer to my prayers," he murmured against her lips.

CHAPTER THREE

Finally, they were alone. The muted sound of party music echoed outside the room. Andre and his people were making sure anyone watching outside get the impression that, like some houses and apartments here and there down the street tonight, people were having a good time, celebrating the ceasefire. There were fireworks and Lola and her two beaus kissed on the balcony, even though, her real one had pulled her back to him quite quickly. Jake made it look like he was eager to go in, but she knew better. Andre only grinned and led them down the hallway and gave them a key before leaving them, whistling loudly.

Alone.

Lola looked around the room with its dark furniture. A man's place.

"I'm sorry it isn't very romantic," Jacob said, standing behind her.

"There are flowers and candles on the dresser," she said, turning to him and smiling. "I know that's from you because I told you I like orchids."

"Yes."

Such small gestures, but it made her heart unfurl with pleasure. "It's enough," she assured him. "I'm just happy to be with you."

He stepped closer. "It's not nearly enough," he said, "but it's the beginning."

She put her hands against his broad chest, smoothing upward, tentatively enjoying the hard strength against her palms. She'd never seen him without his shirt.

"I'd like to make love first before we talk," she finally said, meeting his gaze. His eyes were very blue in the dim lighting. "But first, you must take off that...ridiculous beard."

For the first time that evening, he looked genuinely amused. "It's a good disguise. You didn't even recognize me when I walked past you."

"It was dark," she reminded him, "and...I wasn't really paying attention."

His smile turned into a small scowl. "You were busy with Andre." He finally moved, tugging at her elbow, bringing her even closer. "You would have gone with him."

She realized that he was still edgy with jealousy. It was a new Jake, not just the flirt or the secret lover, but someone who was showing his deep feelings for her. Life with this man was going to be a journey of discovery, of seeing how human both of them were when they were free. She liked what she saw so far.

"It's not a part of my job I particularly like," she admitted, "and it doesn't always end up in sex. You know it's meant to distract and divert attention. I've told you this before. I know it's bothering you now."

"Oh?" He stroked her hair, watching the strands move through his fingers. "Your hair is so soft."

Lola cocked her head. "Don't distract and divert."

A small smile returned to his mouth. "I forgot who I'm talking to." He released a sigh. "All right, I was jealous and wanted to prove to myself that I could make you excited while you were thinking of sex with someone else."

She shook her head. "I don't think much at all. I don't feel at all." She tilted her head back as his caressing hand rubbed the back of her neck. "Except with you. It's always different with you—when we talk or smile at each other or even just a signal, it's different. And tonight, when you finally touched me for the first time, it was..." she paused, closing her eyes and remembering the feeling. She added, very, very softly: "...as if the world receded and only you existed, Jake."

His lips met hers. She opened her mouth invitingly. He didn't hesitate, his tongue took swift possession of hers. It was a lover's kiss—both tender and demanding, taking time to know her mouth and savoring her response.

She opened her eyes when it was over. There was that hungry look in his eyes again, betraying the need she now realized he'd kept so tightly under control.

"Jake, I never would have let anyone touch me in public like that." She licked her lower lip. "You...wanted me to come on that dance floor. I can't believe you put...your finger inside me."

She felt awkward, as if she was a fumbling teenager out on her first date. That provocative intimacy had made her strangely giddy with anticipation, a foreign feeling for her. If he could do that with a touch, what would it feel like when he was finally inside her?

His shoulders shook with silent laughter. "It was just one finger. I wanted your attention on me, only me, and not on your assignment or our observing parties or any other men thinking of how sexy you'd look naked in their arms. No one, Lola, but me. They couldn't see anyway. If you'd come, though, they might have suspected something else was happening besides some dirty dancing. You liked it. All wet like that. I wanted more. I might have put you on the table and fucked you right there in front of all of them."

As usual, he seduced her with his words, making her imagine things. No one made her think of sex the way he did. He made it colorful, the stuff of fantasies. Certainly, no one in this world could make her laugh about it. She gave his chest a light smack, then undid a button on his shirt.

"I'd have stopped you if you had used more than one finger," she scolded. "I'd have made a scene and slapped you or something."

"Two fingers?" He mocked. "In public? How terribly inappropriate."

She undid a few more buttons. Then a few more. Oh my. "Umm."

"What?"

"Your chest is making me think of doing terribly inappropriate things."

His hands slid down her back, pulling the zipper along. Warm hands teasing her skin.

"Let's not talk any more, then," he said, his voice husky. "There is a big mirror and a spacious counter in the bathroom. I have plans for it, terrible plans."

* * *

Lola's dress lay in a pile at her feet, leaving her still in her bra and panties. She stepped out of her clothes and bent to pull the strap off her heels.

"Leave those on for now."

"Your turn," she said.

Lola took a step back to admire Jake's body as he shrugged out of his shirt. She had always like the long and lean look on a man, and she'd always imagined his body as lithe. He'd never dressed well, even when attending expensive functions. It was deliberate, of course. He'd never been a flashy operative because he was so noticeably good-looking already. But only if one looked. Jake Travis always seemed to be able to blend in. With non-descript clothing. With a slouch here. With a beard and cap there.

She stared at the man in front of her now. He was more than lithe and lean. He had the body of a fighter—fit and hard, like a living sculpture. Without his usual disguises, standing here half-naked, casually unbuttoning his pants, he looked nothing like she'd imagined.

If she'd known what his clothes were hiding, she might have seduced him sooner. And no, she didn't care if she sounded shallow.

He pulled down his pants. She glanced down. Nope. From now on her middle name *was* Shallow.

The most beautiful erect penis jutted straight up against his flat stomach. It was golden brown, thick and long, and like most American men, circumcised, its velvety head already gleaming with a tinge of red. She wanted to lick it, to taste Jake. He stopped her as she reached for it.

"Not yet," he said, his voice a little hoarse.

He turned her around to face the mirror. The intense expression on his face made her catch her breath. His blue eyes caught hers in the mirror. Then his hand moved over her stomach and she watched as it slowly slipped inside the waistband of her panties. Lower.

It was all so familiar, yet, totally different. His touch was hotter than she'd imagined. There were other things playing with her imagination. She could now feel his hard arousal pushing into her back as he cupped her. His caress was more intense than her own during their sexy talks. His touch was far more tantalizing than she'd imagined. She moaned.

"This," he whispered into her right ear. "All wet for me."

She leaned back against him as he started to play with her, watching his hand move inside her panties, wanting him to do more.

"Faster," she ordered, impatient now.

"No, slower, remember? Just like our phone calls."

"That's before I saw your cock," she told him.

He chuckled. "You'll have that deep inside you soon enough."

He continued arousing her, sliding sleek fingers against her clitoris, using her liquid desire to bring her higher.

Lola closed her eyes, feeling her insides clenching. Losing control. This was the difficult part.

"I know. You want to turn around and be the seducer. Not. Gonna. Happen." He pushed a finger inside her. Two. He nudged her stance wider. Three. "I've told you. I'll seduce you first. Make you come first."

"Un..." She inhaled sharply as those fingers stroked in and out, over her clit, inside her, over her clit again, round, over, inside, until she felt she couldn't stand on her feet any more. "Unfair."

"Totally," he agreed. "But the look on your face is torturing me, babe."

She opened her eyes and stared at herself. Who was that woman looking back? Her face was flushed, eyes half-closed, lips parted. There was aching desire and lust as her lower body undulated against his hand. He slid her panties partly off with his other hand and she could see how damp his fingers were. She watched as one disappeared and felt it inside, massaging her pubic bone as his thumb circled that sensitive spot right over it. Then his other hand reached over and exposed the hood covering her clit. The thumb slid gently over the sensitive bunch of nerves.

The pleasure was tortuous. She let out a small scream, jerking away. He held her tight as he continued his exploration. Gently but insistently. Barely touching, yet, enough pressure. All along the finger inside her massaged intimately, finding that spot that had her clenching inside, needing something elusive.

It was as if he understood she had a problem with letting go. All these months of flirtation and he listened to her confessions—what she liked and how she wanted it. He knew they were just fantasies because she'd never had it done to her; she'd never been the one taken. Now, he was making her fantasies come true.

"Like this. Look how wet you are, my love."

Her mind dazed by sensation, she gazed into the mirror. He slid her panties down and bent her over slightly. Automatically, she grasped the edge of the counter, still watching, wanting him to hurry. His erection pushed against her soft and eager opening. She couldn't see him, but it felt huge and hard as he finally entered her ever so slowly. She could feel every inch of him, her muscles resisting and easily giving in as he took possession of her. All the while, his fingers kept stroking her higher, pulling at that tension that needed release. His penis, thick and demanding, pushed harder, urging her legs wider.

One shallow stroke in from behind. Gentle brushes on her clit in front.

He pulled out. Pushed in deeper. Gentle, gentle torture of her exposed clit.

Lola lost it. All she could feel was what he was doing.

She whimpered as he pulled out again. He slid in even deeper, a long smooth glide that drew out the urgent

117

sensation begging to free itself. She heard herself moaning louder as his fingers did that magic stroking again. She felt him rub a little harder, giving her the urgency she needed. His strokes came a little faster too. She flared out her bottom, wanting him deeper. He complied, pushing in deep and hard now. His fingers rubbed her there rhythmically.

Her orgasm came in one long release. There was no control at all as she moaned, her whole ass moving against that masterful hand, spurting wet desire down her trembling thighs.

Lola called his name. She couldn't hear what he said as he kept taking her over the edge, hard penis pushing and filling her, his talented fingers playing, giving her all she wanted and more. In that position, watching his hands, feeling his hot cock slapping against her backside, everything seemed magnified. Her final control cracked and she lost her grip of the marble counter as she came again, gasping his name in one ecstatic sigh.

* * *

Jake carried her to bed. There was the satiated glow of a satisfied woman in her smile as she clung to him. It wasn't enough. He wanted to give her so much more, this woman who had haunted him with her sad stories. For years, she'd lost control of her sexuality so she took back power by denying true pleasure in the act. That she'd chosen him to finally be herself humbled him.

He wanted her more than anything in this world. That was why he devised this plan for them. She trusted him, even knowing very well what would happen if they failed. *She wanted to be with him that much, too.*

Knowing that gave him power and he knew it, and he had the responsibility to make sure Lola was happy. Tonight, their first one together, he planned to make her the happiest she'd ever been, give her pleasure and love, share himself and his body with her.

Setting her on the bed, he took off her high heels, taking time to stop and kiss the arch of one small foot. He nibbled upwards, pausing above her mound, inhaling deeply.

"Lola's scent," he said.

Lola's hands massaged his shoulders sensually. "Come up here and give me some more Jake," she ordered.

He laughed. "Yes, ma'am." He climbed over her and kissed the top of her breasts, jutting out from her bra. He bit at the front hook and popped it loose. Her breasts, beautiful small globes, spilled out. "I want to savor every part of you."

He took one tempting rosy nipple into his mouth, gently suckling her breast. She leaned back into the pillows with a sigh.

"I want to savor you," she said, "but this feels...ahhh..."

She shuddered at his love nibbles. He reached between her legs to find her sweet spot again.

"Only after you've come for me about ten times," he told her.

She gave an incredulous laugh. "Ten? Why ten?"

That was his own private fantasy. "That's the number of times you owe me for the phone calls. I told you I wanted to see you come after each time," he reminded her. "Well, you're paying tonight."

Wide-eyed, she studied him for a moment. He continued nuzzling her breast, while his fingers parted her labia, readying her. They have had words. Lots and lots of sexual talk, whispered over the phone. The danger of being caught was just as real then as now, but now that he had her in his arms, finally doing everything he'd narrated...

He would take the time for her to find pleasure. There might not be another time, but at least they would have this one. He sat up without warning.

* * *

"I can't..." Lola couldn't even imagine having another orgasm. It felt wrong. Forbidden, almost. She'd always been the one who gave pleasure, to make the other person weak for more. "I don't think..."

He rose up suddenly, catching her by surprise. He caught her outstretched hands above her head, circling her wrists in one of his.

"What are you doing?" she asked.

"Making sure you can."

There was a click and Lola yanked at her hands. Where did he get the handcuffs? There was a wicked glint in the blue eyes that met her shocked ones.

"Jake!"

He swooped down to give her a quick hard kiss.

"You can. You will." He slowly slid back down to her breasts. One hand returned back between her legs and leisurely parted her again. "Now, where were we? Orgasm number two, wasn't it?"

"Jake!" She protested again, pulling at her handcuffs. It was scary and exciting. She wasn't sure she was ready for this.

"Babe, get ready to be seduced all night long. Not by my words any more. But like this."

And Jake stopped using words.

CHAPTER FOUR

Lola woke up slowly. Sunlight streamed in gently from the crack between the curtains. It wasn't the first time she had done so in an unfamiliar room, but it was definitely the first she'd slept through the night with a man and found herself smiling the next morning.

Jake's arm lay possessively over her middle, drawing her closer when she moved. He felt hot against her. She turned her head so she could look at him sleeping.

Life was so strange. She couldn't have imagined this happening—wanting to stay in the arms of a man, an operative from the opposing side, at that, and being happy. Feeling loved. Jake had practically worshipped her all night, taking his time to give her pleasure.

After the fourth orgasm, she'd lost count. Time was meaningless. Just Jake and his loving. Heat suffused her as she recalled how much she'd enjoyed the night. His hands caressing her. His tongue owning her over and over. And when he'd driven into her with his cock, it was the ultimate possession because he'd made her wait, teasing her while making her come, until she'd finally broke free of her loose cuffs and climbed on top of him and practically raped him.

He'd laughed out loud then. She understood—he'd wanted, to drive her crazy with wanting him, and having no other thought than making love with him.

Giving up control and liking it. Letting go of her tightly-reined emotions. This was all new and surprisingly empowering, as if she'd regained something lost. She'd wanted something for so long. Jake had shown her a little bit of what it was.

"Can you come once more?" he kept asking.

"You never wait for the answer," she panted out, after another mind-blowing orgasm.

"Because you taste so good." He thrust into her. "Because it feels so incredibly good when you're coming while I'm fucking you. Let me show you."

And later still...

"Jake...Jake!" She remembered moaning his name, straining against her cuffs, her legs over his broad shoulders.

"Take all of me, Lola," he'd said.

He'd leaned over, pushing her hips higher, and the new angle was another way to tease her sensitive flesh. It was like drowning in the deepest well of pleasure.

And even later still...

The deep, deep orgasm that accompanied the use of a small egg-shaped vibrator he'd placed inside her, while he loved her with his tongue. She'd never ever forget that sexy mouth of his, moving voraciously over her clitoris as the vibrating tension built inside. She'd wept from the tortuous excitement of being so close to gratification. And when he'd finally slid inside her, she'd gasped and shook while going over; he, too, had joined her pleasure, their frenzied orgasm rocking the bed.

She grinned. They almost broke the bed.

The hand around her waist moved. Cupped her.

"Can you..."

His sleepy voice had the effect of sending her into lust. She was in so much trouble.

"If we keep doing this, we'll never get out of bed," she warned.

"What's wrong with that?"

He turned her around and she lifted her face for his kiss. It was long and satisfying, shared between two lovers who had shared an unforgettable night.

"Nothing wrong with that," she told him, "except it's morning."

It was time to get back to reality. Morning meant pretending last night was just another night for her.

Morning meant going back to her hotel and resuming her role.

She fisted Jake's erection. It was hard and ready, demanding her attention. Was there...

The door to their room open. "Time to get up!" Andre nonchalantly walked into the room, shirtless. "Okay, not that kind of getting up, amigos. I had a wild night and don't need another threesome, thank you very much."

He studied the bed and whistled. His grin was very male.

"Right," he continued. "Looks like you two had a wild night too."

Lola scooted a little lower under the sheet barely covering Jake's and her body. Andre continued standing by the bed, hand on his hips. His jeans were low-slung, showing off enough skin to reveal he probably wasn't wearing anything else underneath.

"Get out of here, Andre," Jake ordered gruffly.

Andre shrugged. "Need to keep up with the act, old man. The black van is still outside." He sauntered to the windows and swept open the curtains. He leaned out the window and yelled out a cat call. "Good morning, crazy world! My buddy and I fucked a wild lady last night! How about you, you assholes out there?!"

There were cat calls back from the streets and across from the other apartments. A few honks from below accompanied crude remarks.

"Oh yeah? Fucking ten inches, you jealous asshole," Andre yelled back. At another male remark, he returned another insult. "She's hot and ready for more. Meanwhile, you can kiss my ass!"

He turned, shucked his jeans down and mooned the world, totally uncaring of the two occupants in the room. He laughed at the howls from outside.

"Take that, fuckheads," he continued, this time a few notches lower.

Lola laughed, amused. She liked this Andre, even though he was obviously doing this as an insult to her handler's men who were outside. He was also quite a looker without his shirt and...pants half-way off. He certainly didn't mind strutting around like that. She glanced up at Jake who didn't seem affected by his friend's antics.

"He's all show and no tell," Jake told her, "so you'd better stop looking."

She cuddled closer to his male heat. "I can look all I want," she said, pertly, "as long as I got this to touch."

She laid a possessive hand over Jake's crotch. She figured everything hidden from view so her naughty touching would be a secret. Jake's reaction, however, brought a snicker from Andre.

"Fucking go away already, 'Dre," Jake turned in bed slightly, adjusting the sheets. "We'll be up soon enough."

"Looks like you're up already," Andre countered, stalking off toward the door. "Be quick, love birds. Weapons to locate, people to trick, and all that good stuff."

He closed the door behind him. Jake pulled Lola on top of him.

"Now where were we?" His half-sleepy eyes were laughing. "Oh yeah, you taking advantage of me all morning."

Lola laughed. Happiness. And a sexy man under her. She could get used to this.

* * *

As expected, there was a message at the desk waiting for Lola when she returned to her hotel. She was to meet with her man at 4pm at a nearby café. Interesting choice.

She was glad it was later in the day. She had some time to freshen up and compose herself. She'd caught herself smiling now and then. That wouldn't do at all.

A bath, a careful pick of clothes and a small lunch, and she was back in form. She went to the market again, picking up some other touristy items for sale. The scarf and glasses stall was empty, which both disappointed and relieved her. She really wanted to see Jake again but that might also be distracting. Perhaps that was why he wasn't there. Or perhaps he and Andre were going over the final details of how to implement the plan now that she'd given them the coordinates of the "aid mission."

It was no secret that thousands of Russian troops were "vacationing" in Mariupol or nearby. Some were already fighting alongside the Ukrainian rebels in Donetsk, but there were some waiting in the sidelines as the governments negotiated in Kiev. Her assignment was to give one message to the troop leader and then be off, but today, she had new information to add to that.

Even though the residents were basking in the hope of a true ceasefire, Lola could feel the tension in the air outside. The sun was shining, the city was conducting its normal business, and people were out and about, but the undercurrent of anxiety was apparent on some faces. There were too many eyes in the city, watching for anything out of the ordinary to report back to their respective handlers. She had a good alibi and her paperwork had been checked, but she hadn't been allowed out of the city yet, which meant, they were watching her too. So her night of partying had been reported, and her current date noted.

Ivan, the man she was to meet, was tall, blonde and clean-cut. She sized him up covertly, noting the way he dressed and how he perused the card menu while sitting like he wasn't comfortable at a table. A man used to long bouts in the field, she decided.

"That was a loud and long party you were at last night," Ivan said, sitting back and watching her. His eyebrows shot up. "Two men?"

Lola gave him a small smile. She picked up her cup of expresso. "Just having fun. Glad to know I'm noticed."

"By everyone," Ivan said, dryly. "Have some of the pastry. It's very good."

A show of small talk was important.

"Why this café?" she asked.

"It's been swept. No bugs," Ivan replied. "The owner is one of ours."

"Ah."

"But it's always polite to be good customers and enjoy this beautiful city." A cynical look came and went from Ivan's face. "Things could change, you know."

Of course. The city would be under siege at any time.

Lola finished her pastry. "It's very good," she said, politely.

Ivan cocked his head. "Not flirting with me?"

She cocked hers. "Not on my orders."

"Do you really just follow your orders every time?"

She had been. But not for much longer. "Don't you?" she countered lightly. "I'm not a sex machine, Ivan. I only do what is necessary to get a job done."

Ivan looked cynical again. "I've seen it. It must be a good job to stay that long last night." He studied her. "Pretty face. Big innocent eyes. Pouty mouth. A tempting package. I've been told it's your usual protocol to leave early in the morning."

Lola picked up her cup and looked over the brim. She was used to being tested. "There were two of them, Ivan. It takes twice as much...work."

The other man leered. "I see."

"Besides, they were drunk Ukrainian volunteers on leave. They told me some interesting things." Lola paused, as if considering something. "Perhaps you'll hear it later since I have to debrief to my handler first."

"Why do you say I'll hear it later? What information did you get from our drunks?"

She paused again. "I've only been cleared to tell you about the weapons coming your way, not about other weapons."

Ivan reacted by sitting up straight. "Other weapons," he said, a thoughtful look entering his eyes. "You mean, you have some information about weapons our Ukrainian side is also receiving. From whom? Not from us, of course. From NATO?" When Lola shrugged, he continued, "From the US?"

Lola shrugged again and sipped from her cup. "I can't confirm. Besides, everything needs to be checked out, right?"

Ivan snorted. "It'd be too late by then. The weapons would have been distributed and our advantage of having more arms gone. You have to tell me now."

"The information needs to be vetted," she argued. "If it's wrong, then what? The blame falls on me. Look, I don't have a direct line to my handler. When he calls or sends a communication, I'll pass on what was told to me. It shouldn't take long."

"No." Ivan pulled out his cell. "He isn't my fucking handler so I have a direct line. We'll get his okay right now and you'll tell me what you know. I don't want to have to meet you twice and waste time if they're smuggling in new weapons."

Lola stayed still, quietly picking up another pastry and nibbling on it, as Ivan made his call. They'd been conversing in Ukrainian but now he reverted back to Russian, barking out his demands like someone used to getting things done his way. Her handler appeared to be doing a lot more listening than talking. Then Ivan finished the call and looked at her. She finished her sweet dessert.

Her throwaway cell phone buzzed barely a minute later.

"I didn't tell him to call you," Lola said before her handler spoke. "He doesn't seem to understand you need to verify anything new."

"You shouldn't have made the slip about the men last night being Ukrainian soldiers."

"I said they were drunk volunteers on leave," Lola corrected. "He made the inferences himself and wouldn't let the matter go when I refused to confirm or deny his questions. As I see it, he wasn't interested in whether I do my job right." She gave her host a steely glance, challenging him, as she continued, "I don't feel I've done enough to verify the information. I was waiting for your contact to see if you needed me to do so."

"How would you do that?"

"I know where to find them. Perhaps meet them again and ask more questions?"

127

"Too suspicious. You have to hatch out a better plan with Lt. Ivan and have him call me with it. He wants to be hands on with this particular mission. If it's weapons, perhaps he's right, time is of the essence."

Lola pretended surprise. "Oh." Inside, a small feeling of jubilation unfurled.

* * *

Jake looked up from the laptop, his fingers finishing up the sentence he was typing. Andre was standing by the door, a thoughtful look on his face.

"What?" Jake asked, saving the file onto a tiny thumb drive.

"You really trust her to pull through."

He pocketed the drive and then inserted another thumb drive into the laptop. "I expect her to try her best." He knew it wouldn't be easy for Lola but the information she was passing on was real enough and her side would have found out later. He just wanted them to have it sooner. "You yourself told me nothing's guaranteed. We can only try to achieve our objective with the tools given."

Andre crossed his arms and leaned against the wall. "Are you calling your Lola a tool?" He mocked. "What is in this for her? What did you two negotiate?"

Jake activated the program in his drive that would eat and break the information he'd been typing into little bits of nonsense, which would then be rewritten over. He scooted his chair back and got up, heading to the sink with his empty cup.

"Stop baiting," he chided mildly, turning on the tap and rinsing his cup. "You know she's more than that to me."

"Yet this is a huge sacrifice on her part if anything goes wrong, bud. I'm curious. Is she on our side? What's she doing?"

"Why all the questions?"

Andre straightened from the wall and walked to the table, giving the laptop a cursory glance. "I'm the inde-

contractor here, remember. I know there's always a pay-off besides the goal of the operation."

Jake put away the cup. He considered Andre a good friend but even secrets stood between friends in this business. He'd hired the other man to delay the Russian "humanitarian aid" convoy because he couldn't be there himself. Lola's role was none of Andre's business, but his friend deserved an answer of sorts.

"Our relationship is complicated," he said. He returned to the table, sat down and studied the computer screen. Lola and he were trying to simplify everything, that was all. But he couldn't say that. "We've agreed to this as one last thing we'll do for each other."

"What? An exchange of traps?" Andre cracked his knuckles, then sniffed. "I can smell your bullshit all the way from here. Look, I'll find a way to delay that convoy while the powers-that-be negotiate this landmine of a truce but you're also releasing information of the whereabouts of weapons from our side. Weapons which I delivered, if I may add, which would really piss me off if they were taken by the wrong parties. I have a reputation to uphold."

Jake chuckled. "From one bullshitter to another, that pile you just dropped smells worse than mine. No worries. You're so full of it, your eyes will turn brown and everyone would know your rep is worth the payment."

Andre never stored any deliveries in one place. He would never share that information with a client, even a good friend. He was just worried about Lola's ability to manipulate and maybe, as a friend, he was also worried about Jake.

"So, we wait," Andre said. "I fucking hate waiting."

"That's why you aren't the spy and I am," Jake pointed out. "Things will be happening soon. You'll be near the border looking for the weapons they're trying to deliver while their main guy will also be busy looking for ours. Delay accomplished."

The delay tactic wasn't going to last long, but that was what his orders were. Perhaps those who were negotiating would put the time bought to good use and not play too many political games.

"We are nothing but pawns," Andre agreed, reading his mind. "They use us and throw us away, so make the best of it while you can, my friend. Don't sacrifice your girl. I like her very much."

Jake smiled as he finished his task. "Not going to and you can wipe that lust off your face. You can't have her."

Andre shrugged, a big grin forming. "I was even willing to go threesome with you, asshole, that's how much I wanted her."

"No dice. I'm not sharing and she isn't willing."

"Oh, come on, she kissed me this morning!"

Jake gave him a heated look. "She kissed us. That was to show our affection for her. It was an act and you know it."

Andre sat back smugly. "She tongued me longer."

"Fuck you. I'm not going to fight you just because you're getting cabin fever," Jake tossed back. "Go find Mariana. She was still hot for you this morning."

His cell phone rang. He exchanged a quick look with Andre before answering it. It was Lola. He nodded at his friend's knowing leer.

Jake easily reverted back to his previous night's persona. "Lola, baby! Are you missing me already?"

As he talked with Lola, he watched Andre stretch, then pull out his tablet to punch some communication with his people.

Pawns were on the move.

CHAPTER FIVE

Lola grinned at the two men in the huge master bathtub with her. All the taps in the room were turned on and the sound of running water echoed against the walls. It was big enough for four people but Jake and Andre were big men and left hardly any room for her to stretch her legs. As it was, Jake had his possessively over hers, making sure no part of her body touched Andre.

Andre just laughed and winked at her.

"Jake doesn't want to share me," he informed her.

She'd laughed at that, curling up closer to Jake. It felt so good to be with him again. She'd missed him desperately. How could one miss another so much so quickly?

"I don't want you to catch his cooties," Jake said, then leaned back against the tub, one hand massaging the back of her neck.

"I've convinced Ivan I can't wear a body wire because I'd be naked and that you two love showers. The cell phone he provided has a special GPS that sends a signal to his men so he'll know exactly where we're going."

She'd written a note to let them know Ivan intended to use some kind of laser microphone to catch their conversation when they were traveling. Jake seemed prepared for this. Just in case, it was already in use, he'd led them into the big bathroom where they'd stripped down as they pretended to be enjoying themselves. Music blared out from the bedroom. Meanwhile, the few people who appeared to her to be Andre's employees sat near the windows, talking and laughing. To any eavesdropper, it would sound like another party going on in the place.

Jake nodded. He kept his voice low. "This room has rippled window panes to make it tough for bouncing airwaves."

Of course, the running water added to the distortion. Still, they delivered any important messages in mock whispers

She couldn't help but feel impressed at how prepared Jake was with the whole operation. She wondered whether this location was a CIA safe house, which would explain all the enhanced tech features. She glanced down at the few pages handed to her, protected with plastic. A short script and some details of their journey ahead.

It wasn't too different from the plan she and Ivan had laid out. She was to "persuade" them to help her out of Mariupol by falsifying papers. She was desperate to get back to her sick relative near Donetsk, exactly where they're heading. If they were to refuse her, she was to drug them and Ivan and his team would take over the questioning, after dispensing with the other partiers in the apartment. Option B wasn't a good one, since the objective was to be led to or near the weapons pick-up point. Of course, Lola knew Plan B wasn't going to happen, anyway, but she went along with the preparations of which drug to use on her "targets."

"We're going to be busy, darling," Jake said aloud, "because we're going back to fighting. We can get you out of here but we have a timetable. We have an important errand to do on our way."

"Oh, can't you take me with you there? I'll be quiet and will stay out of the way." She smiled naughtily up at Jake. "Think of all the fun on the way there. Me, between the two of you."

Andre snatched her papers from her and glanced at the notes. "Nothing about this in here," he stage-whispered, mockery shining in his eyes.

Lola just rolled her eyes and sunk lower in the tub. "Let me persuade you now," she breathed out in her best Marilyn Monroe voice and put her hand between Jake's legs. He was wearing his underwear but the bulge was hard and ready. She slipped her hand inside.

Jake bent his head and kissed her on the forehead. "That's very naughty."

From the other end of the tub, Andre sighed. "I'm being ignored," he protested loudly, then stage-whispered again. "I can add to the script too!"

Lola stuck her tongue out at the other man. She felt very comfortable with his teasing. She slowly worked Jake's erection in her hand out of his underwear.

"We need to pass some time," she whispered, then said in her normal voice, "Watch first, then...maybe you'll agree to take me along."

Jake hadn't said anything at all so far. She grinned up at him and added, "Hmm. Won't you take me?"

"Good Lord Almighty," muttered Andre, standing up and climbing out of the tub. "You two are killing me."

She watched him as he strode wet and half-naked out of the bathroom, yelling at them, "Hurry up. Yo, where are my women? I want some sexy ass right now!"

The door closed behind Andre, leaving them alone.

"He's not pissed off, I hope," Lola said.

"Nah. He's gone off to sex up two of his lovers. Typical Andre. Continue," Jake ordered softly, "persuading me to take you. I am the main driver, you know."

Lola pulled the lever that let the water out of the tub. "Well, then," she said, looking at Jake's hot body slowly being revealed by the disappearing water. "I think my mouth will start persuading you now."

Persuading Jake ought to be a full-time hobby if they ever got out of this alive. Tasting him, watching his body tightened under her ministration, feeling his control snap and taking him over the brink. It had never been this intimate, this satisfying.

"I'll take you," he told her huskily. "I'll take you anywhere you want."

She found out later he meant to keep his promise in many ways. While drying her off later, he bent her over and took her hard and fast. And then against the bedroom door, while they were dressing. She couldn't get enough of him. She wanted him inside her, touching her intimately, and most of all, she wanted to come with him thrusting hard and fast into her. It drove both of them into a frenzy.

When they walked out together, Andre was waiting for them on the couch, still half-naked. A topless woman was curled up against his lap, asleep. His hand was inside her short skirt. Another was also dozing, sitting on the floor between his legs, using his thigh as a pillow.

He shrugged at them. "I had to keep busy," he explained. He was totally at ease, like a man used to orgies.

Lola just laughed.

"Party over," Jake announced. "It's time to get back to work, buddy."

* * *

The ride out of Mariupol was smooth but once they reached territories being fought over by pro-Russian and Ukrainian forces, they had to negotiate through several checkpoints. The road to Donetsk was a lot rougher, with the smell of gunpowder and smoke in the air.

Jake had all the necessary papers ready for both him and Lola. As usual, Andre and his people were prepared, even calling the security at the checkpoints by their personal names. Questions were asked about any new fighting. There might be a truce, but there were still pockets of bloodshed.

"Sergey Prokofiev International Airport," one of the guards told them, shaking his head. He accepted the cigarette from Andre. "Not good. The 80th Paratrooper Brigade has been trapped there since the old terminal fell. I heard through friends the Russians are in there killing them one by one."

Jake frowned. "The elite 80th? Any rescue missions ordered?"

"They're surrounded. There are Russian weaponry flying above and moving around them. They're done for."

The guard shook his head again. "You say the young lady is heading to Donetsk. Are you sure, miss? I don't think this truce is going to last very long, I don't care what those politicians are yammering about behind closed doors."

"Just close to there. I have to get to my sick aunt," Lola explained. "She told me they've already bombed some chemical plant in Donetsk and she's just too ill to get away on her own."

The soldier laughed. "Ach, that was us, bombing the crap out those rebels. We were just exchanging artillery fuck-yous', miss."

"So damn sure the ceasefire agreement won't hold, eh?" Andre asked.

The man spat. "Our men are trapped in there. We're just waiting for more firepower and then we're going in and getting them out. You get your aunt out, miss. Best of luck."

They saluted and went through the checkpoint.

Lola pointed to her cell phone on her lap. "Ivan can't hear but I'm sure his men are tracking our way around this territory. Where are we heading, anyway? This isn't the direct road to Donetsk."

"Scenic route," Andre replied.

Jake looked out the window. This was once a beautiful scenic drive, weaving through lush forests and valleys. Much of it had been destroyed by tanks and bombs.

"A castle," he told Lola. "An enchanted castle. Everyone should get married in one."

Her face flushed and she looked out of the window. "You keep making these marriage hints," she said, softly.

Was his bold, sexy spy blushing because he wanted her as a bride? He found the idea even more enchanting.

* * *

Lola traced her new name on the false papers. Ivan hadn't bothered to ask what name she would be under, hadn't even considered that an important factor in his determination to locate the weapons and get them out of the hands of the "Ukis," as he called the Ukrainians. Only she and the two men on this crazy road trip knew.

The look on Jake's face right now gave her butterflies in her stomach. Marriage. She couldn't even think about it without behaving like a schoolgirl. So she changed the subject.

"Are you as sure that the Minsk Protocol won't stand as that trooper predicted?" She asked. "Maybe the fighting will stop."

Okay, probably not. After all, her side was smuggling in weapons across the border through an aid convoy. Andre shot her one of his now-familiar cynical glances that lit up his eyes with mocking laughter. She made a face at him.

"Let's hope it does," Jake said. "We can do our part and delay the battle. That's all we can do. The rest...."

She studied her man as he grew quiet. He'd told her the job, as he liked to call it, had been weighing on his shoulders the last year. He'd started his career in Intel to stop terrorist violence against his people, to protect innocent lives. Now, it was short term "tasks" for international groups and political players who were brokering power. She'd understood. This wasn't the war he signed on to.

For herself, there was no choice before. She'd been taken from her family and trained, had grown up in an environment that wasn't particularly hopeful. *Do it and your family would be fine.* That had been her first encounter with the bartering of favors. Slowly, her life had turned into a series of orders, which she'd followed because at least she was traveling and seeing new things. But, after a while, even that hadn't stopped her from feeling empty inside. Until Jake. And now, there was another choice. And maybe, even marriage. She allowed a little smile at the thought of herself wearing white and holding flowers.

"We should be there soon," Jake interrupted her reverie. "We're stopping there long enough to let Ivan think we're loading up. I'm sure that would give his GPS a definite location and he'll be sending men after us and our truck."

Lola nodded. "Yes, seizing the truck means adding to his arsenal. The rebels would love some American weapons."

"Yeah, you should be far away from here by then since we're taking the truck the opposite direction," Andre said.

"Will you be okay?" Lola asked, worried.

"What, you suddenly care for me, sweetheart?" Andre grinned. "We'll be fine. The truck is made to drive by itself, like one of those new cars."

"Oh," she said. Self-driving military truck—that was new.

"It'll be mounted with automatic weapons," Jake explained, "and at the right time, it'll explode. No weapons for Ivan. It's all been arranged, Lola. Bodies, news items, everything. I've taken care of the details. I'm the contractor, remember? I deal with of all that stuff for a price."

Lola nodded. Jake certainly had thought of everything to cover their tracks. She must remember to ask him how much money this had cost him. She wanted to pay her half of it.

"Meanwhile, I'll be headed to where I'm sure Ivan's awaiting the arrival of his convoy. The delay at the first checkpoint should be starting the moment the first truck tries to go through. By the time I reach him, he should be getting that news. I have a few embedded agents who will brief me about the situation," Andre added. "I'm sure he will be a pretty frustrated guy for a while."

Lola mentally crossed her fingers at that summation. Ivan hadn't struck her as someone who would patiently wait for things to happen. From watching him yesterday, it appeared he and his team of "vacationing" troopers were eager to continue disrupting the peace process by aiding the rebellion. However, if it's a delay that NATO wanted, then perhaps her role to help avert outright war wasn't a bad thing.

Andre made a turn down a rugged stony road, driving around a man-made column of bricks. Lola caught her breath at the sight of the castle rising upwards, its turrets jutting out atop magnificent old trees.

"Ohh!" That was all she could manage as they drove up the long driveway. It was hidden away on the hill, like a fairytale castle.

"We're going around the back. There might be a few tourists in front but I doubt it, what with the unrest in the country," Jake said. "We need you to move around with the cell phone while we get the other truck ready and then we can tuck that in it. Andre and I are going inside to pass on some communiqué. Do you have to call your handler?"

"No. All is set, he said," Lola told him. She looked at her phone on the seat. "It won't take him long to get the coordinates once the signal settles. My orders were quite clear. Stay in the truck when the weapons are being loaded to make sure that is the truck and to keep you guys distracted."

Jake smiled at her intimately. "You're doing an excellent job with the distracting. Give Andre a few minutes in there to make his call, then come on in. I've something to show you inside."

"All right. I'll take the phone for a walk."

Lola watched the men disappear behind a huge oak door. She pulled at the knot on her scarf, loosening it from her shoulders, before sliding out of the truck to stretch her legs. Slipping the phone in her pocket, she took a quick walk around the old fountain nearby. There were hundreds of coins at the bottom. What would she wish for? Love? No, she got that. Safety. She groped around and pulled one out of her pocket, almost dropping the phone in there. She rolled her eyes at her carelessness and was about to put it back when she noticed the pulsing red light flashing.

It hadn't done that before.

Her breath caught as realization dawned. Bits of conversation zapped like lightning through her mind, things which she had missed during the run-through with her handler.

Ivan wasn't *waiting* for the weapons. He didn't *want* the weapons in Ukrainian hands. The word he used was *"destroy."* And, she realized now, he didn't have to wait for the weapons to be in his hands to achieve that.

She threw the phone into the fountain and started running toward the castle.

"Jake!" She screamed, her heart dropping like a fifty kilo weight around her ankles. She stumbled, got back up and raced towards the door. Everything was happening in slow motion.

"Jaaaaake!" Her scream echoed in the courtyard, in her head, in her heart.

* * *

"What is it?" Jake asked. Andre was frowning and asking odd questions as the talked on his satellite phone. "Bad news?"

"Not sure. My inside man reported that Ivan hasn't moved his position, meaning they're still hanging around near their secret base just outside Mariupol. He should have gone off to Donetsk by now to sign papers as the convoy arrives. Also, I thought he would send some men out in the field as they follow our GPS signal and stay close enough until we have the weapons. They're no-fucking-where close to us at all."

"Huh. Any theories? You think they aren't buying we're decoys?"

Andre shook his head. "Can't tell. My delivery isn't until tomorrow after our little play-acting is over, but I might change the date. But what the hell is Ivan up to? He's definitely the guy needed to run that operation back at Donetsk and if he's late, that humanitarian convoy would head off to the next checkpoint and he'd lose his hidden cargo. I know he doesn't know the UN is going to delay his timetable by parking and searching those trucks for as long as possible."

Jake glanced at his watch. There wasn't much time to make new plans. "So what is all that GPS about? He wanted to keep tabs on Lola and us and..."

They both arrived at the same conclusion and mouthed it out together.

"Missile!"

At the same time, from outside, Lola's scream rang out.

"Lola!" Jake ran toward the door separating them. "Andre, warn the others!"

"Head for the back!" Andre yelled back. "Everyone, go down to the cellars. Or the dungeon! Get down under the damn castle!"

Jake didn't have time to look back. He flung the door open and found Lola on the threshold. He dragged her inside.

"GPS is for tactical attack now," she panted out, trying to explain.

Jake pulled her along behind him. "Hurry, hurry! Come on, we've got to go down to the old dungeons."

They scrambled after the few agents who had been there to help. Andre was at the top of the opening.

"Move!" he yelled at them.

They all dove down the crumbly flight of steps. The loud crash of iron-cast door followed behind them. Everyone ran as fast as they could.

"Move, move, move!" Jake ordered. "We need to get behind the second door! Hurr—"

A huge blast interrupted his words, shaking the castle to its foundation. There was a huge whoosh of air as they reached the second door. Most veterans knew what that was. Backfire.

Jake pushed Lola through. He could feel the heat coming down like a hurricane. Lola turned and grabbed him by his shirt, refusing to let go. Someone behind them screamed as he became the first victim.

Andre slammed the heavy iron opening shut. Jake pushed Lola onto the ground and covered her body. A huge sonic boom sounded and the metal door groaned and bent ferociously. A huge bolt flew out. Someone else screamed. Jake kept Lola under him, protecting her with his body. What felt like a huge wave of heat pushed against his back.

Don't let her get hurt. Please don't let her get hurt.

* * *

It was dark and hard to breathe. Lola coughed and tasted grit in her mouth. Dungeon dust and some horrid bitter blend of smoke, fire and debris. She coughed again, trying to lift her head higher, but Jake was heavy and not moving.

Not moving. Panic assailed her again.

"Jake!" She croaked out his name, choking from lack of air and dust. He didn't move. The panic grew full-scale. She tried to turn, squirming and pulling, inching herself out from the weight on her, calling his name over and over.

Finally, he stirred and groaned. "I'm okay," he said. "Just knocked out for a moment."

"Listen up! Get up when you can," Andre called out from somewhere to her left. "It won't take long for the authorities to arrive. Those of you who are capable must take charge. Petrov!"

"I'm alive," a voice called out.

"And able?"

"Yes."

"You have to round up the uninjured. Someone check on those who are down."

"I will," Jake said, slowly getting up. He bent and helped Lola. "Are you all right?"

She couldn't see his face in the semi-darkness. "Yes," she assured him.

"Oh, no, you two come with me," Andre ordered. "We're getting the hell out of here before the media descends and the melee starts. Petrov, you know what to do!"

"Yes, sir!"

Andre was suddenly in front of them, holding a lantern. "You two aren't injured, I hope. I need you able and running. We have to get away now." His voice was crisp, a far cry from the mocking tone he always adopted. "I have a delivery to oversee. I have a beef with that fucker Ivan now. He thinks he could just bomb a castle and get away with it? Did you fucking know about this, Lola?"

She shook her head, then realized he couldn't see her. "No." Her voice was still hoarse from swallowing dust. "I truly thought he wanted to get his hands on the weapons for himself. The advantages of showing off UN weaponry while both sides are talking are too great, and our side would have a better control of the negotiations. But Ivan isn't one for negotiating, I suspect."

"I guess not. Fucking guy just about started a war all by himself," Andre said. "Jake, we have to go to Plan B."

"All right," Jake said, by her side, his voice low. He whispered in her ear. "We're out of here. With our new identities, no one will say anything. The old Jake and Lola have been killed. Are you ready for the next step?"

Lola stared up into his shadowy face. It was now or never.

"I love you," she said, simply. "I'll go anywhere with you."

She came so close to losing Jake. Her own life meant nothing without him. Besides, it was quite clear that she had just been thrown away by her side, used as a sacrificial pawn for their next big move. She wasn't bitter. Far from it. They'd just set her free.

He hugged her to him and she breathed in his scent and his heat. She didn't ever want to be parted from him. She squeezed him hard.

"We aren't out of danger yet," Jake said, quietly. "I tried to cover every possible angle while getting the job done, but didn't think of this one. If the missile had hit with you out there..."

His arms around her grew tighter, as if he would draw her inside his whole being. She understood how he was feeling. It had almost been over.

"I'm alive," she whispered. She ran her hands across his back and started. "Why is your shirt wet? You're bleeding!"

"Really?" Jake released her, looking over his shoulder. "It's not hurting."

Guiding Andre's hand so his lantern would give her better lighting, Lola stepped around to examine Jake's back. Andre whistled.

"There's a rip in your shirt, bro," he said. "Don't move."

Lola carefully lifted the red-soaked material. She could see raw skin here and there but there weren't any deep injuries. The tightness in her throat eased a little.

"I don't see any puncture wounds," she said. "It's more sticky than wet, like your blood is drying."

"I think the heat from that missile burnt part of the shirt off his back. Look, the material is scorched here and there." Andre lightly pressed in a couple of spots and nodded as Jake reacted to his pats. "Yeah. Lost a few layers of skin like a bad sunburn, bro. Lucky bastard."

Lola shivered. It could have been worse. Losing Jake while he was protecting her. That would have been unbearable. She covered her mouth to contain a small sob.

"Shhh." Jake turned. He took her hand in his. "I'm alive. I love you so much I'd do it all again."

"Okay, love birds, it's been a blast, but let's go, hmm?" Andre urged. "This old place has some tunnels dug out of the dungeons in World War II. Follow me and you two can do all that kissing stuff once you're outside away from here. There'll be a fuck-load of people descending here very soon. We need to implement our plan now."

"We're right behind you," Jake said. "Ready?"

Lola looked up. To her, his smile seemed to light up the whole place. He was her knight in shining armor, rescuing her from the dungeon that was her life. She smiled back radiantly.

"Ready," she replied, giving his hand a tug.

They walked out of the chaos without looking back. Nothing behind them, everything ahead.

*E*PILOGUE

*E*very Russian could quote Pushkin from childhood. He wrote some beautiful love poems which I'd dismissed as trite and silly. There was no such love that he celebrated about, mourned over, yearned for.

Until Jake.

His love elevated my life and my being. His presence in my life shone like the sun over the former shadows that had been eating my soul.

From the very day we'd escaped, taking the old hillside path outside the tunnel, he'd been mine. We'd turned to look at the billowing smoke over the bombed out castle, so damaged by Ivan's attack, with the sound of air raids and sirens in the distance. Rage had filled my heart to see such destruction. Another emotion that had been frozen inside me all these years.

"We'll build our own castle, my darling," Jake had said, in Russian, wiping the tears that had somehow leaked out of my eyes.

I smiled at that promise now. Our very own castle wasn't quite the size of a three-car garage.

Jakiv and Lynda Zukovich lived in a very small apartment in a rural town in Switzerland, but with our new names and papers, our simple life was like a fairytale to me. Jake had a stash of money he'd been keeping and we lived on it for a while until we'd settled down in our new country.

We didn't communicate with the outside much. As far as I knew, the old Jake and Lola had been reported among the dead in that burning castle—there were international articles about two tourists with their general descriptions reported as victims of the Russian rocket that had taken out an entire side of the tourist attraction. No one had come forward to claim the remains.

The attack did achieve one thing, though. It became part of the excuse to keep the Russian convoy at the border. Humanitarian aid or not, every truck had to be parked and searched by the Ukrainian guards, while being observed by UN officials. I hoped Ivan got reprimanded for getting nothing out of all that trouble he'd caused. That well-timed delay had also given Andre and his men enough time to regroup and the last call we'd gotten from him was just before he'd gone in to rescue whatever was left of the 80th Regiment at Donetsk Airport. The tie-up of the convoys had kept reinforcements from reaching the rebels surrounding the trapped troopers. From the news, it'd been a bloody battle, but many were rescued.

It was all out of our hands now. I only kept up with it enough because one had to keep an eye on the news at all times. I guess I was also paranoid.

As the weeks became months, time had slowed down for us even more. We enjoyed being what we are now—no spying, no information gathering, no telling half-truths.

Once upon a time, I was a sexy agent who was taught to seduce with a smile and a look. I traveled all over the world and sat by powerful men, listening in on conversations. I touched and read documents that the most important rulers of the world would pay top dollar to have a peek. I could call several names on my black book and have them fly me anywhere I wanted.

I gave that all up. Now Jake worked at a farm and I was giving lessons to make pysanky eggs.

"Why are you looking all mysterious and sexy at me like that?" Jake asked, watching me.

I'd thought he'd been sleeping.

> *"And my heart beat with a rapture new,*
> *And for its sake arose again*
> *A godlike face, an inspiration,*
> *And life, and tears, and love, and you."*

I smiled down at him by my side. I did it for love.

~FINIS~

NOTES FROM AUTHOR

I hope you've enjoyed this story. You can subscribe to my newsletter by emailing me at Jenn@Gennita-Low.com. Please write NEWSLETTER in the topic area.

1) The Minsk Protocol was signed in 2014 but did not last. The ceasefire was broken a few months later when both sides resumed artillery fire in the city and suburbs of Donetsk.
   http://rt.com/news/223887-ukraine-army-donetsk-bombs/

2) The bloody battle for Donetsk Airport was of utmost important in the war between Ukraine and the Russian-backed rebels. It was a top-notch, state-of-the-art facility with glass walls and computerized departments. In order to take full control of the city, the separatists had determined that Sergey Prokofiev International Airport must fall. The Ukrainians were cornered in the second and third floors of the new terminal, waiting for help. The separatists, having intercepted and shelled much of the aid coming from the Ukrainian government, killed and captured a number of the elite 80th Paratroopers Brigade. A small group, who managed to hide in the many serpentine hide-outs of the airport, was rescued when international "contractors" aided the Ukrainians. This is all reported in the news. I've just added Andre and his group into the mix.

Today, after several battles, all that remained of the airport is wartorn rubble. Bloody battles continue to erupt around the city of Donetsk, proving that peace treaties are merely pieces of papers ignored by men who are determined to win at all costs.

3) When the ceasefire agreement was signed, Mariupol did indeed celebrate noisily, its inhabitants hopeful that their city would be saved from battle. However, as of March 2015, much of the city has been shelled and many citizens have fled. Many are moving out of the country as refugees.

Gennita Low writes sexy military and techno spy-fi romance. She also co-owns a roof construction business and knows 600 ways to kill with roofing tools as well as yell at her workers in five languages. A three-time Golden Heart finalist, her first book, Into Danger, about a SEAL out-of-water, won the Romantic Times Reviewers Choice Award for Best Romantic Intrigue. Besides her love for SEALs, she works with an Airborne Ranger who taught her all about mental toughness and physical endurance. Gennita lives with her mutant poms and one chubby squirrel.

To learn more about Gennita, visit www.Gennita-Low.com, www.rooferauthor.blogspot.com and www.facebook.com/gennita

Other Books by Gennita Low

BIG BAD WOLF (a COS Commando novel)
(The Prequel to Everything)

~ ~ Hot Spies Novellas ~ ~
DANGEROUSLY HOT
SIZZLE

~ ~ Crossfire Series ~ ~
PROTECTOR
HUNTER
SLEEPER
HER SECRET PIRATE (short story in SEAL of my Dreams)
WARRIOR

~ ~ Secret Assassins (S.A.S.S.) ~ ~
INTO DANGER
FACING FEAR
TEMPTING TROUBLE

~.~.Super Soldier Spy ~ ~
VIRTUALLY HIS
VIRTUALLY HERS

~ ~Sex Lies & Spies~ ~
*novella series
THE GAME
THE PAWN
THE SEAL
THE GAME AND THE PAWN (print)

~Susan Stoker's Special Forces (Kindle World)~ ~
NO PROTECTION

~ ~ Cristin Harber's TITAN World ~ ~
EDGE OF TEMPTATION

~ ~Liliana Hart's MACKENZIE FAMILY Collection~ ~
WICKED HOT

ALSO

~ ~ Children's books as "Gennita" ~ ~

A SQUIRREL CAME TO STAY

NEWSLETTER: Jenn@Gennita-Low.com

TURN PAGE TO READ AN EXCERPT FROM WARRIOR

EXCERPT FROM WARRIOR (CROSSFIRE SEALS SERIES)

CHAPTER ONE

He could hear the story being passed around his team now. The Stooges pretty in pink. The Stooges spent a night together on a pink four-poster bed. The Stooges had pink bathrobes and slippers.

"Ya gotta admit, Cumber, pink is sexy."

"I prefer them on my women, hidden away for my pleasure," he said.

"True, but maybe this room was meant to be inspiring, right, Dirk?"

"Mink, if you're sporting a boner, you get to sleep on the floor."

Lucas Branson, AKA Cucumber by his SEAL team mates, came from a family of warriors. His father was an Airborne Ranger of the 173rd, the biggest, baddest fighting group of men ever. His cousins were scattered around the world, playing war games in special operations and doing what warriors do best, bringing down the enemy. He came from a family of tall men, big hulks descended from, as his father liked to tell him when he was a kid, giants who ruled the earth. And he'd grown up believing his father as he grew up towering over shorter men and taking lessons to become the next warrior-in-line in a family fueled by competition and medals.

And now he was a SEAL, the U.S. Navy's special operations force specializing in sea, air and land where the biggest, baddest group of boys resided. His team mates were his best friends and part of the family, and he didn't let anybody get to him. They called him Cucumber—Cumber for short—because he always kept his cool, no matter the situation.

But not tonight. Tonight, he was thinking about killing his sister. He loved her very, very much, but yeah, he might just strangle her.

He stared up at the bright pink canopy above him with its frilly lace and big bows and drooping flowery shit with children's faces inside them, all smiling down on the bed's occupants. Strings of pink pearls dangled, waving gently.

It had to be a slow death. Because he knew she was laughing her ass off right now. A slow, painful..."

"Hey, Cumber, how big is your dick?"

"I'm in a fucking pink bed with two men in a fucking pink room. My head is resting on a fucking pink pillow the shape of a pink flamingo. I'm not discussing my dick with you."

"But what else can you talk about on a pink bed in a pink room?" Dirk insisted. "Unless you want to chitchat about the pearls and bows. Or the cupids around the pink mirror. I was mesmerized by them while using the pink hairdryer."

Mink sighed loudly. "I need a dose of manhood. Let's talk about Cumber's dick. A huge dick should cure us from an overdose of estrogen. Come on, Cumber, how big is your dick?"

Lucas ignored his friends. His sister...what was the best way for revenge? Maybe he could sit on her till she begged for mercy. Except, she had a black belt and as a big brother, he'd taught her quite a few moves to protect herself. He used to hide her favorite toy, but at their age he needed something a bit more...painful.

"You know he's got the biggest dick of all of us," Dirk said, "so why the need to know?"

"If it's so damn big, why didn't he have the balls to say no to the Pink Room?"

Lucas closed his eyes as his two friends, having made their point, roared out laughing. They were very close buddies—they were often called the Stooges—so close they could ad lib a whole comedy routine without a script on the spot. He'd known one was coming the moment they'd stepped into the Pink Room, the "most popular" suite at his aunt's B&B.

The laughter went on for a good minute, till his friends were holding their stomachs and choking. He lay there, waiting for it to subside. He could turn on the TV, except holding on to a pink sparkly remote would just set them off again. He stared resolutely at his feet at the end of the bed, peeking out of the dark pink comforter. Yeah, if he had time, he'd sew up Lulu's sleeping bag so the next time she went out camping, she would get a nice surprise when she tried to crawl in and stretch out after a long day hiking. Except that kind of revenge took too long to realize. He wanted to get back at her *now*.

"You know, Cumber," Dirk finally gasped out, "when she said, 'The Pink Room will be perfect for you and your gentlemen friends to relax in,' I was having visions of your stately aunt being the madam of a secret boudoir, especially when she added, 'You'll find lots in the room for entertainment. Enjoy yourselves, boys!' I thought maybe she was pulling our legs or something. I never expected *this*!"

Dirk spread his arms out to include the whole room. Mink, lying in the middle, pushed one arm away.

"Watch it. You're encroaching on my pink space."

"Yeah. She gave us one four-poster bed, dude," Dirk continued. "What was she thinking?"

"The place is booked up. This was the only suite available," Lucas said. "My aunt probably thought we would be happy with the biggest room she could put us in."

"Man, didn't she know we sleep on submarines? We can crawl in one of her closets and take our naps there," Mink said.

"Yeah, but we wouldn't be tucked in and enjoying our pink featherbeds, yo."

"Look, I know you two are doing me a favor using our time off to help my aunt and sis move furniture, so I'm taking your digs without retaliation," Lucas said, affecting a yawn. "What's the big deal? Just fucking close your eyes and pretend you're lying in a muddy river already. Me? A bed is a bed. We'll be out of this place in two days, tops. Then we can go party somewhere for 24 hours before we head back. Now turn off the damn lights."

"I can't. I need a drink first to get the smiling pink cherubs from haunting my dreams tonight."

"Cucumber, go get us a drink. You owe us. The pink fridge is at your side of the bed, anyway. And oh, the pink bottle opener is hanging..."

The sound of the door unlocking cut off the rest of Mink's sentence. Lucas turned his head, full attention on the door. Someone outside kicked it wide open. His sister popped her head in and a big flash blinded him.

"Surprise, pink SEALs!" He heard her yell out as she ran off. "Picture is on 'My Friends Space' page!"

Lucas jumped off the bed and chased the shadowy figure as she made off, laughing, down the corridor. He heard Mink and Dirk behind him, following along.

Must get back that camera.

Must. Kill. Sister.

The B&B was a big mansion, with many hiding places. His sister, like Lucas and his team, was barefoot, her feet making barely a sound as she climbed the stairs. He took the steps three at a time, hoping they wouldn't creak too much. The chase must be done on the quiet. They had their aunt to consider. And the guests, too.

Going up was good. That meant she was heading to the private section, away from the guests. The only obstacle was his aunt's apartment also being up here, so if his sister managed to slip in there before he got to her, she would be home free. No way was he going to bother his sleeping aunt, what with him and his team mates shirtless and wearing only shorts...shit...he just remembered Mink had only his underwear on. Fuck. Please God, don't let Aunt Clementine walk out of her rooms. Because he didn't want to explain to the family how a naked SEAL buddy sent their proper, very Southern aunt into a conniption fit in the middle of the night.

Out of the corner of his eye, he saw Mink in his tighty whities scaling to the next story using the wooden banisters. With him snapping at her heels and Mink cutting off her escape route, his sister was going to be trapped between them any moment now. She reached the top of the landing, saw her problem, tried to dive through Mink's legs, got tangled and up-ended him. Lucas heard muffled ouches and oomph's as he reached them. He took a step nearer to apprehend their target.

154

A door suddenly opened and a shadowy figure jumped on top of Lucas' back with a "Hoo-ah!," startling all four of them who were already out there. A puny arm curled around his neck, trying to force him back. The new attacker weighed less than a sack of flour but Lucas realized Dirk, who was covering his six, wouldn't know that. Not wanting to hurt his sister's sidekick, he curled his arms under the assailant's knees, twisted sideways against the corridor wall and sat down, thus imprisoning the assailant. One thing registered quickly. Whoever it was had very nice, silky smooth, bare legs, which were now paddling hard like a panicked creature, trying to kick him. The puny hand around his neck reached down and grabbed a handful of his chest hair.

"Ow!" Lucas growled, tugging at the hand. He slid his hands up from under his prisoner's knees and grabbed a handful of silky smooth ass. His assailant squealed.

"Get off, you goof!" He heard his sister's demand coming from a few feet away.

"No way," came Mink's reply. "I think you have something that belongs to..."

Another door opened. The landing was suddenly flooded with light. Cucumber blinked. Everyone froze.

"Lucas Samson and Lucille Belle Branson! What's going on out here? Oh my goodness! Mr. Mink!"

Lucas closed his eyes. Aunt Clementine in curlers and pearls. Definitely a sight that would doom any warrior's rage.

***